Other books by Advance Concept Design Books for Bryant Val Jeane Faubion:

The Dairy of the Beans
Texas Short Stories

The Second Daisy Queen

by

Bryant Val Jeane Faubion

This is a work of fiction. Names, characters, places, and incidents are products of the imagination of the author, or are used fictitiously, and are not to be construed as real. Any similarity to actual events, locals, organizations, or persons, living or dead, is entirely coincidental.

CID, Inc.
6706 Bar K Ranch Rd.
Lago Vista, TX. 78645

Published by arrangement with
Advanced Concept Design Books, a division of CID, Inc. Tx
Library of Congress Control Number
to be assigned
International Standard Book Number
ISBN 13: 978-0-9799723-1-7
ISBN 10: 0-9799723-1-0

For information, address
bvjfaubion@advancedconceptdesign.com

First paperback printing October 2007
Printed in the United States of America

THE SECOND DAISY QUEEN

by BVJ Faubion

PROLOGUE

The Daisy Queen which is pivotal to our story existed ephemerally in the small, little-known town called Hanghat, Texas. The events leading to the building of the second Daisy Queen, and the effect of its brief existence in precipitating a sudden change in the lives of its townspeople, are outcomes of a series of events which began long ago. So, let us begin at a time in a historical past which, even after daydreaming in highschool classes during our cursory exposure to selected facts in American history, may still give us some feeling of connection and understanding to the events which allowed the sweeping of Hanghat, Texas into existence. You, the reader, like most of us putters-of-eggs-in-one-basket, no doubt, will select one of the events which helped to birth Hanghat and consider it as the seminal root which eventually sprouted the outlandish burg. I, however, feel that one should not go back so far in time as to be unsure of the efficacy of each event in producing a singular outcome. By my reckoning the following historical milestones directly contributed to the existence of Hanghat and the people in it, but not to the existence of the nearby towns of Phleville and Haygap, or the state of Texas. At least I don't think so, unless Texans are living in a state once destined to be called Austinvania.

So, now I begin to explain what I have discovered about the happenings that birthed Hanghat, revealed a secret or two, salvaged a forgotten genealogy, reunited the hearts of two young lovers, and placed windshield wipers on the rear window of a 1952 dodge named, "Hazel."

CHAPTER 1

In the tale of the coming into being of the village of Hanghat, the first egg in the basket, according to my egg gathering, was the expulsion of the French settlers from Acadia. I will not stoop to qualifying the present condition of the world by pursuing the current rage of attributing the inscape of our present societies to a googol of occurrences such as a certain butterfly escaping the darting tongue of a chameleon lurking in a Rose of Sharon shrub growing in Jerusalem in 19 A.D., so, in this narrative of nascence I will not go beyond the year 1759 when the British told our story's pertinent Acadians, "Get out and don't come back."

After that expulsion the next contributing factor of importance was the great-grandfather of a future Louisianan being busy doing his business in the bushes when an Ojibwa war party attacked a group of exiled Acadians in what is now Detroit. Other paramount factors were Napoleon, one of his bastard sons, Spain ceding the Louisiana Territory to France, a hurricane changing course, the runt of a litter of puppies not being sack-drowned in 1839, a lightning bolt splitting and felling a particular tree in eastern central Texas, the Napoleonic Wars, and the timely immigration of Monsieur Eccrine Fissile and his family to the Louisiana Territory the year before it became the Louisiana Purchase.

The Fissile family arrived in New Orleans

in September 1802. The ship they sailed upon was having a rough passage through the Gulf of Mexico when the hurricane heading directly for the shipload of terribly seasick passengers, each wishing they would just die and get it over with, mercilessly changed course toward Mexico, leaving the green passengers tossed and tossing all the way to port.

Eccrine, his wife, Eclaire, two daughters, and a son had departed France so that the son, fourteen years old Clovis, would not be drafted and killed in Napoleon's wars. The family settled into a large house in Vieux Carre which, of course, was called Nouveau Carre at that time, or simply, Le Carre. M. Fissile succeeded in a wine importing business and died in 1830.

Clovis, having a wife and two children, continued his father's wine business. His first son, named Eccrine after his grandfather, was a dreamer with an urge to travel. Eccrine had little interest in the family business which involved the handling of heavy barrels and tedious paperwork in stifling offices in the New Orleans' summers.

Eccrine had inherited his grandfather's affliction of sweating profusely when performing strenuous work or just sitting in a sultry room. He often thought that, like his grandfather, he would someday slip in the wine warehouse in a puddle of his own sweat and break his neck. Consequently, Eccrine became the distributor for the family business, and his brother Fiston, a non sweater, took over the jobs at the warehouse and office.

Eccrine traveled to the towns and taverns in southern Louisiana making sales calls and escorting wagon loads of wine. His constant companion was his dog, Spot. Eccrine had discovered that Spot was a wino when he returned to his meal one noon to discover the dog finishing off the spilled contents of a bottle of vintage 1820 wine. Catching the dog in the act explained the perplexing mystery of whom or what had been the agent knocking over and uncorking previously opened wine bottles.

One day he found that it helped sales to have Spot lap up a saucer of wine in the presence of a prospective client. Eccrine would place the saucer on the floor and declare that Spot would only drink the finest wine, but, in truth, the dog was an alcoholic runt from a litter of foxhounds and would drink any alcoholic beverage presented, or accessible without the need of thumbs.

In the early spring of 1842, before sweating season had commenced, Eccrine, while on one of his many wanderings through his sales territory, met a lovely Acadian descendant by the name of Mademoiselle Overte Plassein when Spot stopped to sniff her butt as she was bent over attending her honeyberry bushes by her front gate. Being French, however, neither Overte nor Eccrine was embarrassed by the event; the only reaction was Overt's startle at an unexpected cold nose.

Overte stood up and turned to see a rider so handsome that her heart fluttered at the same rate as her eyelashes. She smiled, told him how much she enjoyed working with her hybrid berries which were a cross between the golden huckleberry and a native, white grape.

"I grafted them together, myself," she said, "after I came upon them in yon woods," pointing with her trowel as she spoke. "Now they grow in the gardens all around my daddy's yard."

She was one year younger than the twenty years old Eccrine, and they both had noticed that the other had black hair and blue eyes. Overte was doll-like with a small waist and adequate, childbearing hips, which was an attraction to men of that era.

They courted and were married in 1844, settled in the dry upland country northwest of New Orleans, and little Clovis Fissile was born in 1845. Early in 1847 came sweet little Eclaire, who looked nothing like her brother, to Overte's dismay, because Eclaire was a love child with a French lieutenant serving close by in the U.S. army. Eccrine, satisfied in all things marital by his obliging wife, only concluded that his daughter favored her mother's side of the family.

The French lieutenant had at first found Overte to be unresponsive to his attentions, but being skilled in seduction and having a raptorial personality that eventually seized any woman by her libidinal hindquarters, the lieutenant upon a third encounter with Mme. Overte Fissile was soon to be many times in her honeyberry patch, then in a haystack he had, like a bower bird, erected in her backyard, close to a dense thicket offering a quick, unseen getaway.

Eccrine, to further avoid any labor which

dehydrated him to the point of delirium, and at Overte's urging, became a politician. He willingly agreed to follow her suggestions for his future as she molded him into a man of compromise who was often called away from home to attend to political affairs. He never wondered or asked about the always fresh, hay structure behind his house or about the occasional straws to be seen tracked between the back door and his wife's boudoir.

In the autumn of 1860 Eccrine Fissile awoke on a cold, non sweating night drenched from a nightmare about a coming civil war between the North and the South, and, following the family tradition of awaying from war to save a son, he decided to move his family west to Texas.

At first Overte protested, but she loved her fifteen year old son and she began to realize that it might be best to move away from the military garrison which housed her lover. Eccrine was home more often in the last two years and things could become problematic, she thought. Also, the lieutenant had breathily referred to Overte as, Nita Lou, during the neck-kissing phase of his usual passionate outpouring at their most recent, haystack liaison, and that had prompted Overte to suspect he was cheating on her.

In the few months before their departure, thirty families of Acadian descent came to the Fissile home and announced that they also wished to head west to a new life away from the mosquito infested bayous, and that they wanted Eccrine, who had risen to some stature as a politician and getter-of-things-done, to lead them. Among the husbands were many who suspected the lieutenant and wanted their wives away from him. Among the wives were many who felt their luck was running out and that it would be better to put distance between themselves and the garrison's irresistible and profligate devil of pleasure.

Thus, were the causes to begin a journey that would result in Hanghat, Texas, though, of course, other events would have to occur and not occur before Hanghat's name and location would be definite things.

CHAPTER 2

The Louisianans led by Eccrine, who along the way had practiced the art of riding his stallion while sitting tall in the saddle with his chin held high to project as noble a bearing as possible, crossed their wagons into Texas on March 22, 1861.

While they discovered Texas was more populated than they had thought, and began to realize that they would have to go further west than they had imagined, a lovesick French lieutenant providentially drowned in the rain-swollen Red River while following the escaping Cajuns. He was longing for a particular woman—an illness that before this had limited his range of affairs to three miles, or less, with no intervening watery obstacles.

Was the drowning a major, altering event for what was becoming the history of Texas? If the French lieutenant had caught up with the Fissile party, the beans would almost certainly have been spilt. Some psychic child could have hollered, "Papa," and run to him. Various husbands could have noticed that their supposed children carried the same incised, French lieutenant nose upon their faces. The French lieutenant could have suffered a confession episode while standing on a crate in the middle of circled wagons. He had already endured periods of melancholy during which he imagined gathering his gamut of children and current enceinte lovers to lead them to a paradise he imagined to exist somewhere in Florida, a la Ponce de Leon and the Fountain of Youth. Even if he had survived the river but never found the Fissile party, no telling if there would have been replacements for some of the future legends of Texas history as the un-drowned, French lieutenant seduced his way across the region.

And let's mention the gene segment itself which spurred the lieutenant on. The dominant and persistent gene had survived since a time it had first urged males and females within a small band of Homo Erectus's to mate with a different partner after a first child was born. In the female's case it directed them to mate with any male from outside their family, and in the male's case, any new female at least once. The mischievous urge exists in all humanity, but in the French lieutenant and the legendary Don Juan, the gene was hosted in a deviant and exquisitely compelling form which, when activated, drained the blood from the common sense area of their brains and conducted it to their brain's libido region where it placed their silver-tongued persuasive ability directly and relentlessly under the control of their genitalia. When passed on from parent to female offspring, the gene created a powerful urge to not conceive two children having the same father, and no amount of social conditioning could stop the recipient from her appointed rounds.

Another facet of this particular form of the fornication-driving gene was that it compelled its possessor to mate only out of doors, away from the nest, so to speak, in bowers or glens or, as the lieutenant preferred, in well-located haystacks of roomy interior design with small, peak-out slots at all points of the compass. This deviation in the gene from the typical form, which can demand satisfaction even in the bedroom of the cuckolded, had, no doubt, many times saved the lieutenant from being husband-shot; securing the longevity of the role heredity had forced upon him.

The lieutenant, like the men he made cuckolds, were all, in a sense, victims of the peppy, unrelenting bit of what would someday become known as: TAGACC in sequence 1,769,696, or as genome biologists would call it "The Roll-In-The-Hay Deviation."

Yes, the tidbit of code had been strong in Napoleon's bastard son floating face-down toward the Gulf of Mexico, and it had been strong in his mother who had carefully arranged for a romantic rape from the "Little Corporal" who, afterward, had to be helped down from a roof. And it was firmly established in the children and wombs carried by some of the wagons heading west to what was hoped to be a mosquito-less and a French lieutenant-less new life.

The Fissiles, not being pioneers in a true sense, had hoped to settle in southeast Texas so they could visit New Orleans often, but as they searched for available farmland they found themselves further and further away from the relatives they had left behind. Then, about where east Texas became central Texas, their luck changed.

Another event necessary in determining the coming of Hanghat was the drought east-central Texas had experienced for three years. Eccrine's map showed the wagon train to be north of an area of unclaimed land bordering the Bratity river, and the map indicated that they were close to a trail leading into it. Some previous owner of the crudely drawn map had written the word, "swamp," across the trail. The map indicated another way into the area from the east, but that meant backtracking, and men since the beginning of time hated to return for anything.

Assuming a most Napoleonic pose, Eccrine reined his horse to face southward, and he authoritatively thrust his arm out and fingered their direction of travel—the shortest overland, non backtracking, come-what-may route to the new destination. A scout was sent out to see if a swamp was there, and he reported that the map was wrong because the swamp area was dry but filled with a dense undergrowth and saplings.

So, the group went forward to investigate the unclaimed land, and after a day of cutting a trail through a dense tangle of brush and small trees, they emerged to see what looked like a wall of hills in their way, however, in front of them lay the trail indicated on the map. The winding trail led them to the top of a broad plateau bounded by the river and the lowlands they just hacked through. The plateau was about seven miles wide and ten long, and the soil smelled and felt good. They prepared to spend the night and explore the next day. They did not know that the swamp was usually present, and several feet deep at its shallowest, and that the land, besides being elevated, set upon iron deposits, and that these two factors wrung the lightning from any thunderstorms which swept over it.

Indians had considered it too dangerous to live on, and a first attempt by Europeans to settle upon the plateau was abandoned after a month of raging thunderstorms with lightning that killed five people, nine horses and mules, two milch cows, and an assortment of dogs and pigs and chickens. Local lore said the uplifted region was "bad medicine."

The Fissile party had come upon the often malevolent plateau when it was on its best behavior. Not aware of the plateau's past terrors, the party split into groups and wandered about, seeking the best place to build a town, but every possible site seemed not to be as good as a next possible site. They admired the panoramas when they came to the edges where the land rolled gently down to the river to the west and south, and steeply down to the lower elevations of the rest of Heespud County to the east.

The plateau, called the "uplift" by people living close to it, was rolling grassland with wooded areas along shallow ravines and tributaries leading to a creek flowing southerly through wood and field. The creek flowed down the southern edge of the uplift and rushed over a series of small waterfalls to join the Bratity river.

Summer was upon them and Eccrine was

beginning to sweat. They were not close to the rim, which would have afforded a distant view, and there was nothing else outstanding about their locale as two of the men readied their bird guns when Son of Spot went on point. The entire group stood silently waiting for the dog's quarry to appear.

Eccrine, sweating like a dripping faucet, was standing astraddle the trunk of a tree which had been struck and felled by pre-drought lightning. After a bit, the dog came off point and trailed off in the opposite direction. Everybody began to move and talk again, then, as Eccrine stepped onto the sweat drenched log, he slipped and fell hard upon his head. He slowly got up, wobbled, removed his hat, and hung it on a vertical limb sticking up from the log. In slurred, concussion-affected speech the people with him heard him say, "Dese place hang hat," before he went unconscious for three days.

Upon returning to life, Eccrine saw that the others had made a camp and had settled-in around him. Overte, tending to him, said the words, "Welcome to Hanghat, Texas, Monsieur Eccrine."

This is the story of the founding of Hanghat as related in a manuscript, "Hanghat—The Early Years," written by Agnes Roue—one of its original settlers. The handwritten pages were found among the effects of the Jeanette Foudre who appears later in the story.

Thus, on May 14, 1861 Hanghat was founded at a place where no town should have been. But, come to think about it, other towns and cities in Texas came to exist at stark, middle-of-nowhere locations for no apparent reason. The most notable is Dallas—founded by French settlers in 1841. Why is such a large city at that spot? There is no navigable river or confluence of rivers. There is nothing of geographical note. Yes, seemingly nothing to make a small town located there grow into a metropolis. Hanghat, on the other hand, never was to grow beyond a population of 1,300 souls. It had sputters and near misses, but Hanghat's history took place with few outside influences—an always present Brigadoon few were to discover. On a few forgettable occasions, minor events had made the town newsworthy for a day, then it continued, set leaning against time in a chair and busy doing the crazy things Hanghatters had done for years.

CHAPTER 3

Soon, parcels of land had been chosen after much discussion followed by a chance drawing of parcel numbers from a bag, then, finally, by some coin flipping and trading. A committee led by Eccrine registered the claims over at the county seat, and every able body got busy building houses and preparing farmland and pastures. When that first year brought normal rainfall, the swamp returned, and the men had to construct a roadway across it by laying logs, piling mud, and setting stones.

Overte had been promised a house as fine as the one she had parted from in Louisiana, but since there was no brick or sawn lumber available, Eccrine and some helpers set to building a larger than necessary log cabin overlooking the Bratity. The structure set above a grassy hillside leading down to the river just downstream from where the river flowed past the entrance to the swamp.

Over a period of two years the cabin grew to become Texas' first rambling, ranch-style house. It had wings at all points of the compass, and parts of it were three stories tall when the spring rains of 1864 came. The rains were not heavy but they came steadily for several weeks.

The hillside setting below the house and above the river became saturated toward the end of the second week of rain, and, while the Fissiles were in Hanghat at a town meeting, the house was struck and set on fire by an extraordinarily powerful bolt of lightning. The shockwave from the thunderclap so shook the water-laden hillside that its sodden mass liquified and flushed into the river below. For a moment the burning house set on the edge of a two hundred foot, sheer cliff. Then the house and the cliff tilted and wobbled and separated from the rest of the uplift, resulting in a swaying column of house-topped earth which, with the house enveloped in flame, toppled like a gargantuan candle onto the pile of hillside already blocking the river's flow.

Because there had been no torrential rains, the river was not out of its banks, and it did not have the force or volume to carry the hillside and house downstream. Instead, the obstruction remained as a dam behind which the rising water began to flow into the low swampy channel that had once been the river's path before nature formed the bend.

This diversion of the Bratity into the previous channel was another necessary event in shaping Hanghat's future. The uplift was the most western part of Heespud County, but now the river flowed between the uplift and the rest of the county.

Without a bridge the only overland route to Hanghat was across the beheaded river below the mudslide, but this was through Tick County to the west. A bridge, located down river about fifteen miles, already united Heespud and Tick counties. A delegation from Hanghat traveled to the Heespud County seat to tell them what had happened and ask for a bridge. Heespud, however, had no money or desire for another bridge so far from the main road, and the Hanghatters were told to take the long way round and have a nice day.

As for fording the river, it was too treacherous to cross. The Bratity in its geological past had changed course many times to run east or west over indurated beds of rock at the base of the uplift. There were large bowl-shaped depressions in this solid rock that the river had cut into at one time or another in both of its channels around the uplift. These depressions caused the moving waters to roil with swirling and tumbling currents just under what appeared to be a quiet surface. Folks familiar with the insidious stretch of water dared not swim in those parts of the Bratity, and horses and cattle instinctively refused to cross there.

The first history altering effect of the new dam occurred in March of 1865 when a mercenary detachment of cavalry arrived in Heespud County seeking conscripts for the Confederacy. The South was running low on men, and the detachment was being paid five Confederate dollars for every man brought back to the military base at Tyler, Texas. The county's mothers lamented as sons were hauled away, but the mothers in Hanghat were to be spared the tragedy.

After scouring the eastern reaches of Heespud, the detachment attempted to ride to Hanghat, but the soldiers found a river between them and what the county census indicated as a town with possible conscripts. The zealous officer in charge ordered his men to follow him as he spurred his wild-eyed mount into the lurking turbulence. All but one rider entered the river. Private First Class Wimpler's horse, new to the strict do-or-die discipline of the cavalry, refused to even set one hoof into the water.

Wimpler, also having good, horse sense, did not want his mount to respond to his urging, and he only lightly kicked its flanks while a ghastly spectacle began to happen before his eyes. He sat quietly in his saddle and watched the gray opaque water carry the line of mounted riders downstream while rising and falling currents repeatedly brought each rider to the surface and then sucked him down again. In a circling eddy they appeared as riders on a deadly merry-go-round. Then, released to continue in single file, the emerging and submerging figures appeared to be parts of a single, undulating, Chinese dragon until, finally, each rider and horse disappeared under the water for a last time.

Wimpler returned to the county seat where a fellow soldier detained captured conscripts. He told the story of what had happened to the detachment and told his companion they might as well forget about it all and free the conscripts; which they did.

No other press-gangs ever showed up in Heespud County because the war ended just a month later, but, at the time of the event, Private Wimpler, seeing his chance, deserted the Confederacy to reappear in history thirty-one years later in Paris in the company of Oscar Wilde who was infatuated with Wimpler and fascinated by his gothic poetry about drowning.

CHAPTER 4

After the loss of their log mansion, Eccrine and Overte Fissile and their two children moved into Hanghat. The town consisted of only a few log cabins and three larger structures built of logs and rough-split boards—the general store, the Fissile wine warehouse with adjoining tasting room, and the town hall which also served as the schoolhouse and church where semi-Catholic services were held every Sunday, even though there was no priest present. The Fissiles lived in the tasting room until June of 1864 when lightning razed the town hall and the wine warehouse. The Foudre family, who operated the general store, accommodated the homeless Fissiles until the first wagon loads of sawn lumber and four crates of lightning rods arrived in September of 1866.

All Hanghatters had many times needed lightning rods, but none were available during the war. Within two days of delivery, every cabin, barn, chicken coop, and outhouse had at least one rod on top. Most Hanghatters, not wanting to be struck while in a vulnerable condition, placed lightning rods atop poles spaced along the path to the outhouse.

The wine facility was rebuilt with sawn lumber, and the Fissiles included living quarters above the store.

Life changed for the Fissiles when Overte's father, Augustin Plassein, died and left his estate to his only child. The couple then built what was to become the grandest house ever in Hanghat. Built of red brick, it was two stories with four attic dormers and a steep roof line. It had green shutters, windows of glass shipped in from Galveston, and two white columns fronting a circular driveway. The family moved into their new house in 1868.

Another big event for the Fissiles that year was the marriage of Eclaire to Sans Foudre—owner of the general store. A sad event for the Fissiles was their son's departure for California with a bad case of go-west-young-man fever.

The Fissiles also sponsored a new church complete with a bell tower topped by a cross which was also the uplift's largest lightning rod. The interior was decorated with statues carved by Don Roscoe Coupable, who was a boy of sixteen years when his family made the trip to Hanghat with the Fissiles. He had sat in the church basement while he carved life-sized wood statues for the new church. He had completed three before lightning struck him for the second time. Both strikes hit him while he was on his way to work in the basement, and after the second bolt Don Roscoe felt certain, without knowing why, that the strikes were signs of God's disapproval of the statues.

After Don Roscoe's first electrifying episode, his mother, Laverne, a cellist, giving thanks to God for sparing her only son, heard a heavenly voice tell her she must leave the uplift and return to Louisiana to mend holey mosquito netting for the poor.

After the departure of his mother on her mission of mercy, and that second brush with death, he carved a fourth figure, then departed the uplift to live somewhere else. He had mentioned Montmartre, but no one ever heard from him again.

His work had included sitting figures of Mary and Joan of Arc greeting worshipers in a two-font vestibule. Mary appeared to be cradling a baby Jesus in her arms, but the baby was not present. The Joan of Arc had full, almost puckered lips, and held her arms as if welcoming all to enjoy the rapture of the church. Inside the chancel in a niche to the left of the altar there was a statue of St. Thomas the Doubter kneeling upon a prie-dieu with his elbows on the shelf and his hands supporting his chin. The statue's eyes looked forward as if Thomas was listening or daydreaming. An empty chair, carved and set in place by Don Roscoe, set in a niche to the right of the altar.

The sculptor had departed before the last figure had been set in the vacant chair. The figure was stored in a corner of the church basement. It had never been displayed because the pose suggested that Don Roscoe had been working on a statue of Mary Magdalene at work with her legs wrapped around a client, her left hand holding a missing goblet of wine, and a look of ecstasy upon her upturned face.

The ladies of the congregation were relieved to know that the client and goblet were nowhere to be found, and they concluded that Don

Roscoe had departed Hanghat before those items were carved.

Photographs of the church building indicated it was of sufficient size and quality for the diocese to begin sending a priest to Hanghat every fourth Sunday. That practice continued until 1880 when the circuit priest suddenly quit showing up. Pleas to the diocese for his return were answered with the explanation that Hanghat was too inaccessible, and the population would have to attend church fifteen miles away in Tick County. The resulting neglect by the diocese caused Hanghatters no alternative but to continue self-service in their ornate but priest-less church.

Hanghat continued to grow in population from within. Only thirteen outsiders moved into the greater Hanghat area during the 1870's. Jeanette Foudre, complete with the Foudre family birthmark, a brown diamond shape of about 125 carats on her left thigh, was born to Sans and Eclaire in 1872.

In 1874 Eclaire gave birth to Jeffie Foudre who was fathered by Charles Habile, a son of you know who—for the time being, let's just refer to him as FL. Jeffie seemed to have escaped any of the possible physical evidences of inbreeding, even though she had a same grandfather on both sides. She carried a birthmark on her right thigh, but it was shaped like a question mark. His second child luckily looked somewhat like Sans, which was fortunate because Sans had some suspicions about Charles Habile; suspicions which the comely Eclaire easily convinced her uxorious husband were unfounded.

CHAPTER 5

Hanghat's business center grew to extend along a main street for several blocks. After a number of side streets were formed, the main street, as was the custom of most every growing town, became Main Street.

The town was still isolated from the outside world because a single dirt road, which crossed the previous riverbed, was often muddy and impassible. Officials from the county seat had never come to Hanghat because of the sixty-mile round trip extending through Tick County. There were periods as long as a year when Hanghatters would see no strangers in town. A wagon departed Hanghat and traveled the riverbed road once every two weeks to deposit and pick up mail which was placed by a postal carrier in an outhouse-sized shed at the turnoff from Tick County Road 4.

With only the occasional new male, of any species, coming to the uplift, inbreeding began to show its effects in people and animals. A year after the Fissile's arrived, a great granddaughter of Eccrine's original Spot, a family pet named Spot Girl, had birthed a litter of fourteen which were adopted by other Hanghatters. Soon, every dog in town and on the uplift farms carried a large black spot on its left side, and each of them had the word, Spot, in its name. There was Shep Spot, Rover Spot, Spot King, Spot Boy, and on and on. Burned Spot had pulled an infant from a house set afire by lightning, and Cold Spot had survived a week of being lost during the Blizzard of '68.

Livestock were also exhibiting inbreeding's effects. Cattle would be seen gathered all facing each other in a circle where they would moo for hours. At other times cows would walk in columns of two or three, like soldiers, or form a single rank to graze across pastures from one side to the other.

As for human inbreeding, the fecund non swimming FL had fathered twenty-six of the children who began the trip from Louisiana, of whom eight were yet to be born—two were born on the journey. By 1880 there were seventy-five relatives in the uplift who had no idea they were related. Kissing cousins who were much more than kissing cousins unknowingly married each other, and in 1890 their number grew to 132.

On occasion some Hanghatters did wonder and discuss why so many of them had the same Moliere-like sense of humor. Also, FL's overly-intimate nature manifested itself by producing curious personal and social behaviors in his offspring; behaviors of which some spread through social interaction to Hanghatters who were unrelated to FL.

Soon it was normal for the uplift's people to stand less than two feet apart during a conversation. The occasional stranger in town would feel uncomfortable and apprehensive to be approached so closely. Not only would the Hanghatters stand face to face, but, while so doing, also had the tendency to stare at the confronted speaker's mouth and chest.

Another disconcerting but not communicable habit pervasive in FL offspring was a peculiar, distinctive snicker which was barely audible and would often sound at unfunny times. The habit went unnoticed by locals, but it led outsiders to believe the snicker was affectation or sarcasm. Combined, the eccentricities caused visitors and traveling salesmen to talk about the strange ways of the short French people over in Hanghat, and outsiders decided that the Hanghatters were just behaving in the "French way," and they showed each other French postcards which effectively demonstrated a reason for Hanghat's peculiarities.

FL's descendants preferred to eat in silence and considered conversation as an interruption in the forking and chewing process. Once a meal began, the typical FL descendant got down to serious mastication and was unresponsive to questions and even requests like, "Please pass the salt." While eating they seemed to completely lose awareness of others, and this behavior was learned and imitated by unrelated Uplifters.

FL relatives were also obsessed with the desire to be seated. They never stood around. When not forced to stand while at work or play, they were sitting on the ground if no seat was available. People could be seen sitting all over the uplift. In town they sat on steps, hitching posts and rails, fences, buckets, large and small stones, and each other if there was nothing else to suffice. They would sit and talk in non sequiturs.

Statements like, "It sure is the nice day I ate breakfast at school there's a new teacher my red hen had chicks today," could be overheard. These behaviors spread through social interaction to all Uplifters who didn't want to appear abnormal, resulting in twit-like behavior in all the children and most of the adults—related to FL, or not.

CHAPTER 6

Young Jeanette Foudre worked after school in her family's general store. She was intelligent, observant and well-read, and had a keen interest in biology and botany. She had shining black hair and blue eyes and soft feminine features except for her chin which was a bit too strong for the rest of her face. When her hand was covering her chin, as it often did during contemplation, she would appear as adorable and possibly coquettish. With her full face in view she was seen as less feminine, yet, still quite agreeable to the eye.

Jeffie was a pretty girl whose moon-shaped eyes and continual smile gave her a constant look of awaiting an imminent and delightful surprise. She took pride in her bright brown hair, piling and fluffing it until, from a distance, it would seem to be a small bear cub riding cuddled-up on her head. Jeffie also worked in the store, but only three days a week when she would sit on a barrel she rolled into position to stock shelves, or dust the displays, or take money at the register. Jeffie read a lot of magazines, but few books.

In her job at the store Jeanette casually observed that many Hanghatters of her generation had similarities in appearance and mannerisms. At Hanghat public school she became aware of those same qualities in many of the youngest students. In her last year of school, inquisitiveness had led her to think something very strange was going on. Encounters and conversations with individuals in other towns reinforced her theory that people on the uplift were collectively weird. Without much further thought, she concluded that the area was just full of people emulating each other's behavior because it was such a closed society. Or, maybe, it was the water, she finally told herself.

In 1890 at the age of eighteen, Jeanette departed for college in the East. She majored in biology and studied the works of Charles Darwin and Luther Burbank. By her senior year, studies in phylogeny had revealed which specific resemblances in a group correspond to relationships and common ancestors, and which resemblances were merely learned behavior.

She began to ponder the similarities demonstrated by many on the uplift, and she would often think about their outlandish mannerisms. "My god," she exclaimed one afternoon in the university library as she visualized a Hanghat family elm tree in the middle of Main Street with a laughing man at its base throwing attributes up into the branches where a tree-load of people sat snatching them from the air and gobbling them up.

Jeanette graduated in biology in 1894 and returned to Hanghat to teach in a new larger school and to delve into what her educated mind told her was a genealogical mystery. She moved into a two-bedroom home next to the school and immediately began her detective work before school started in late September.

Jeanette turned twenty-two that summer.

She gave much attention to, and spent much time with Jeffie, who pronouncedly possessed the snicker trait. Jeanette was to begin her investigation by scientifically observing and recording her sister's mannerisms.

Jeffie took delight in the new interest by Jeanette who had in the past neglected her younger sister's companionship, choosing instead to spend her time reading and being annoyed by Jeffie's interruptions in her routine. That is, Jeffie enjoyed the attention until the discovery of the journal and its comment about "...a subtle snickering occurring at the oddest times."

On that afternoon Jeffie confronted her sister, telling her that she had no such snicker and had never had such a snicker in her life. She said all she had to say while her face was just ten inches from Jeanette's. As Jeffie spoke, Jeanette was calculating the spacial distance between them and taking note that her sister only looked at her mouth while she berated.

Then Jeffie revealed something to her sister that instilled alarm and dismay. Jeanette at first refused to admit to the preposterous allegation, then Jeffie began to give examples by mimicking her sister's voice and mannerisms.

After her parody Jeffie departed with a final, "So there, Miss Know-it-all. You've snickered and talked in everybody's face since I've known you . . . and you're the biggest sitter in Hanghat."

Jeanette was still sitting where she first took refuge from the accusation that she now realized was the truth. She stared at her image in the vanity mirror. She pretended her reflection was another person, and she began a conversation during which she purposely emitted the dreaded snicker. She now knew that those who possessed that telltale, heredity revealing feature effected it unconsciously. She moved forward to only inches from her reflection and spoke and snickered. Alarmed, she realized she had been a party to conversations with the opposite sex while standing too close for propriety. She blushed in the mirror and felt shame as she thought of what her professors and others at university had thought about her eccentricities. Why hadn't anybody told her this before? She looked in the mirror at her lips and evoked the snicker.

"I'm a twit," she said to her image. "Say it mirror. You're a twit."

Tears ran as she cried, then she caught herself and, staring at her image, forced a hearty, self-mocking snicker. Her mood shifted as she began to see the humorous aspect of what just had seemed so dire a problem. She snickered into the mirror; the snicker grew into a giggle, then she stood up when her giggling grew into laughter that ended with a snort.

Jeanette thought of how true it is that we cannot see ourselves as others see us. She wiped away the tears of laughter below her eyes, and blotted her chin of those first tears of discomposure, stood up and adjusted her dress. She bravely went to her journal and began to write a list of her own mannerisms from as distant an objective view she could achieve. She wondered who that mysterious progenitor could have been and she renewed her determination to uncover him.

While Jeanette was in the midst of her endeavor to correct her display of unwanted mannerisms, Don Roscoe, hoping that God was busy somewhere else, sneaked into Hanghat. He came on horseback with a large bundle strapped across the horse's rump. He carried the bundle into the church basement where he placed three objects into an empty chest.

After hiding the chest from view, he removed the blankets covering the suspected figure of Mary Magdalene, kissed its cheek, crossed himself, and prayed. He then replaced the coverings around the figure and set it on top of the chest. There, far back in a corner of the basement the objects would set until discovered years later.

Don Roscoe Coupable thought that what he was doing could, surely, be against God's wish, but the love of the memory of his mother compelled him to challenge the lightning and to complete what he had begun. His plan was not to directly defy God by placing the statue in the church's empty carved chair, or installing the objects he had brought with him. He would let those acts be accomplished, or denied, by God's will.

It was a star-filled sky he rode under as he hastily retreated from the uplift, sitting low in the saddle, expecting at any time a star to throw a bolt of lightning, petrifying him.

Don Roscoe then traveled to Louisiana where he was to invent the world's first rotating mosquito swatter.

CHAPTER 7

That 1894, before school commenced in September, Jeanette returned to working in the Hanghat General Store— which was the store's new name. Her father had also made the store into a post office, and, since there was no postal delivery, all of the Uplifters had to drop off and pickup mail at the store. Jeanette had assumed the job in her family's store to facilitate her research by observing the mannerisms of the customers. Besides, she felt an obligation to help her father who had been upset by a recent series of lightning bolts that came close to him, but, as usual, had zigzagged away from where he stood.

The game was afoot, and she was a graduate biologist on the trail of a person she referred to in her notes as, Sire. Sans and Eclaire had told her to spend her summer relaxing and preparing for her teaching position, but she persuaded her parents that it was her duty and pleasure to help with the store.

Jeanette waited on customers and relentlessly engaged them in long conversations after which she would sit behind the counter and write her observations in notebooks. Once a week she and Jeffie enjoyed the wagon trip to the mail shed at Tick County Road 4.

When not working, Jeanette would visit people at their homes, bringing their mail as an excuse for dropping by. She made great effort trying to not be obviously gathering information, and when she thought she was suspect of being nosey, she would interrupt the conversation with stories about herself. She went to every farm on the uplift and by summer's end she had spoken with and observed the mannerisms of about every adult and child in the area.

It was on a Monday before noon when three older ladies came unexpectedly to Jeanette's door. She invited them into the parlor where they sat while she prepared tea. From the kitchen she could hear them conversing in agitated low voices. She overheard one of them say something about Jeanette having knowledge about their secret. When she returned to the parlor to ask if they wanted a snack with tea, the women quickly ceased conversing and appeared ill at ease, and the same occurred when she entered with the tea tray.

Each visitor sat in silence and sipped tea as if all their concentration was upon the cup in their hand and the act of bringing it to their lips.

Jeanette, the only one speaking, commented on the weather and how lively the bird songs had been all summer. Jeanette began to feel ill at ease; suspecting her interest about local family ties was about to be questioned, somehow, as to her motives.

Mrs. Terre Mouvoir cleared her throat and said, "We three ladies share a heavy burden. One we wish to remain a secret, at least until after we pass on. We do not know how much you are aware of, but your questions have led us to believe that you have been told our secret or, at least suspect what it is."

The other two ladies nodded agreement, then, cued by nervous tension, everybody at once raised their cups and took a sip, then, like a synchronized tea drinking team, the cups all returned to the saucers with a single, clink.

Silence ensued, during which time Jeanette decided to not even flinch during an expected second round of precision cup lifts, sips, and saucer returns.

Mrs. Collage then said, “It all began in Louisiana before we came to Hanghat. He was very persuasive. We could not help ourselves.”

Mrs. Mouvoir interjected, “Let’s not go into particulars, Mrs. Collage.”

The visitors then sipped again, but that time it was a wave of motion as first one cup, then a second, then a third cup was raised above its saucer, sipped from and returned in reverse order.

Jeanette struggled to retain her composure, and sat concentrating on not letting her expression transit from a subtle smile to an open mouth laugh. Attacks of the giggles had been considered a character flaw by her rather Victorian teachers at university, and she had engaged herself in sessions of self-control which had to some extent been successful in lessening the frequency of her sudden outbursts.

Then, losing the battle, she burst with laughter. Tea squirted from her nose.

To save herself from embarrassment, and her visitors from feeling slighted, she laughed the words, “I just thought of a joke a customer in the store told me Saturday. I’m so sorry, ladies.

Please, please forgive me."

Through tears of laughter she saw a blurry vision of her three visitors all simultaneously lift their cups and hold them above the saucers. Then, she fell out of her chair in a continuing fit of uncontrollable giggles.

Mrs. Collage set her cup and saucer on the coffee table, and then aided Jeanette back into the chair. The older woman wiped dribbles of tea from Jeanette's mouth and chin and said, "I'm sure we would like to hear you tell the story. Maybe, dear, you should save the joke for a time when you can tell it without falling onto your floor."

It now seemed to be Mrs. Habile's turn to speak. She cleared her throat and said, "My dear, we know what you studied at university, and we know the questions you have been asking. We don't know what you have learned about us here on the uplift, but, if you would, please keep any conjectures to yourself, lest they upset others and cause broken hearts."

Jeanette agreed to quit asking questions for the sake of the community and to keep her conjecturing to herself. She was pleased, however, to know that her research and conclusions had led her so close to the truth. She wondered about the man who had been mentioned.

The ladies were on the porch when Mrs. Collage turned to Jeanette and whispered, "Dear, you will have to get control of your emotions if you're ever going to be a success at retelling humorous stories once you've recalled them."

For the rest of that summer, until late at

night when hers was the only lamp lit, Jeanette would study and sort her data. The writings contained in her five notebooks would have seemed to most people, at that time in history, to be the work of a madwoman, but any modern sociologist or anthropologist would have recognized studies in behavioral psychology and proxemics and metalinguistics. Jeanette recorded the spacial distance separating people during discourse (passionate and dispassionate) as well as how they spoke and moved, acted and reacted, and how and when they laughed or snickered. Her community's silent repasts especially intrigued her.

On the morning of September 10, 1894, Jeanette laid a completed genealogical chart onto her breakfast table. The assembled pieces of paper showed the lines of familial connection and suspected familial connection for the populous of the area. She had assigned numbers representing the sum of the subject mannerisms in each individual. The numbers indicated occurrence of the behaviors to be most pronounced in her parent's generation. She noted that Jeffie's number was higher than most, and she saw that for some young children the number was from middling to small, even to zero, but high in many—as high as her sister's number.

She poured a cup of tea and sat down by the chart. Mrs. Collage's statement supported the information indicating that the progenitor and done his work in Louisiana, up to the time her grandparents had departed for Texas. She surmised that whoever he was he had impregnated her grandmother, Overte. She wondered about Jeffie's having all the Sire's characteristics. Did she and her little sister have different fathers?

The last entries in Jeanette's notebooks were assumptions about the Louisiana Don Juan, the provocateur of passion who had caused all this. The one who had seduced so many women including her grandmother, the staid and family loving, Overte Plassein Fissile.

In December Jeffie was married to Baptiste Collage, and both, sitting on high stools, snickered during the civil wedding ceremony held in the church which yet remained priest-less.

Jeanette was opposed to the marriage, but she could not say why, because to say that she had evidence that Baptiste was a relative, based upon her comparative studies of eccentricities, would alienate her family and, no doubt, cause repercussions throughout the community, or, as she sometimes feared, make her look like a meddling busybody. She sensed that, behind her back, she was already known to be, at times, a giggling idiot.

CHAPTER 8

Eccrine and Overte often entertained at their grand house. The house set on a trail which had become known as Fissile Lane, even though there were no street signs in 1894 Hanghat. The well-maintained dirt carriageway ran east for half a mile from the north end of Main Street, then circled into the Fissile driveway.

Jeanette and Jeffie visited their grandparents often, and both enjoyed attending their grandmother's parties where different small groups of Hanghatters were invited throughout the year. Twice a year all the people of the uplift were invited to an all day festival. These grandest of parties were held at the beginning and end of farming season.

It was September 22. The summer crops had all been harvested, and the autumn party would begin at noon. It was nine in the morning, and Sans and Eclaire had arrived with their daughters to help Overte with the final details for the party.

By noon the guests, each bringing a chair of some sort, had begun to arrive in carriages and wagons which were parked in the field across from the house and along the road. Everybody noticed a stranger ride in and dismount. Then, all watched him walk up to Eccrine Fissile and introduce himself while standing what the Hanghatters considered as a great distance from Eccrine's face. This was the first anybody in the uplift had personally laid eyes on the mouth and chest of the towering five foot ten inch tall, Bob Beer.

Bob, needing a hideout, had heard about the rarely visited Hanghat from a man who had demonstrated his knowledge of the place while giving a French postcard presentation. So, knowing the folks in Hanghat were of French heritage, Bob introduced himself as Robert DeBiere. Bob, possessing social skills and wit, was quickly accepted as a guest, and he moved about the yard among the array of lightning rod poles, introducing himself and entering into conversation. Within five minutes the observant newcomer had ceased maintaining that era's standard, three foot spacial separation, and he was standing an uncomfortable eighteen inches from others as they conversed with him. He did his best to generate impressions of himself as humble, honest, intelligent, but found it difficult to concentrate while thinking that some kind of stain or imperfection was on his clothing, because everyone he engaged in conversation would stare at his chest.

After a guest told him the story of how the Catholic Church had abandoned Hanghat, leaving the town with a church but no priest, Bob added piety to his list of desired first impressions, then, as "Reverend" DeBiere, he explained how it was that he was a Lutheran minister who was searching for a flock.

A crowd carried their chairs over and sat down around this likeable man of God. When somebody asked if the Lutherans had confession, Reverend DeBiere corrected any possible misconception his potential flock had about the details of his denomination.

"I am of the new Lutheran Catholic faith. We not only have confession, but, also, for each and every soul there is a one-on-one connection to his God, which all can share."

A buffet was declared ready, and with full plates and glasses the guests retired to their personal chairs where they ate in silence. Bob Beer at first didn't notice that he was the only one to continue talking while eating, but no one sitting close to him even looked up or nodded when he declared for a second time, "This is certainly a fine meal." Then he asked, on a second attempt at recognition, "Don't you agree?"

Moderately chagrined and feeling like a first time visitor to Rome who had not learned all of what to do when in Rome, he ate his meal while listening to a mocking bird's song intermingled with sounds of chewing and swallowing and implements scraping platters. When people were away from their seat, and standing in line waiting for cake, they spoke to each other, but as soon as they had cake in saucers they would clam-up and return to their seat and eat without comment.

The period of silence was over when conversations abruptly began to spread, as in a flock of birds beginning to chatter after a perceived danger had passed. Feeling it the proper time, the reverend got up from the chair the hostess had lent him. He climbed onto it.

Standing there he spread his arms and proclaimed, "Never has an unexpected guest been made so welcome by a host and hostess and their dear friends. Thank you all very much, indeed."

The party was a great success, especially after Reverend DeBiere had informed all present that Lutheran Catholics were allowed to dance while sitting, and drink wine till the cows came home, and that a few of the Ten Commandments had been toned down a tad, made a bit more specific, and less applicable in certain circumstances.

Overte then came forward and told the reverend that her house had never been blessed by a priest or a reverend, and she asked him if he would be so kind as to do that for her.

The Reverend DeBiere turned and faced the imposing structure. He lifted a mug of red Bordeaux from the hand of a woman sitting close by, and he approached the house's two columns in a slow deliberate manner.

There he turned his head upward gazing at the bulk of the building and said, "Ut cumque placuerit Deo usque ad nauseam, requiescat in pace. Fide et amore fiat voluntas tua. Amen," which translates as, 'Howsoever it shall please God, even to the point of nausea, rest in peace. By faith and love, Thy will be done.'

He then splashed wine on the base of each column, signed himself, chugged the remainder of the wine, and turned to face the seated crowd who all signed themselves and then cheered.

Eccrine and several other prominent Hanghatters came over to the reverend, then after a short discussion, Eccrine announced that the reverend had agreed to hold services for the community on the following Sabbath.

Jeanette had watched the Bob spectacle from beginning to end. She had seen Bob's picture in last week's mail pickup. It was tucked in her current notebook—an exact likeness of Bob Beer on a wanted poster which read, "WANTED by Heespud County for Flimflam and Repugnant Behavior. $25 REWARD."

She let Mr. Beer have his moment, then, while she hesitated to expose him as a flimflammer sought by county authorities, she began to think of how, at least, this was a male of marrying age who was from another family tree in a separate woods. As a biologist she began to perceive Reverend DeBiere as a husband for some Hanghat lady—DeBiere, an ex-flimflammer who was once repugnant but who could in the future become a dedicated husband and father to a non-snickering, non non sequitur delivering covey of kids.

His future depended upon his reverendly answer to her one question. As the party ended and guest departed, Jeanette went up to Bob Beer and asked, "Are Lutheran Catholic men of the cloth allowed to take a wife?"

"Yes, indeed they are, ma'am," he replied.

"Welcome to Hanghat Reverend DeBiere," she said loudly for all to hear. Then moving her lips close to his ear, she whispered, "Robert DeBiere. That's French for Bob Beer. There's no way I'll ever let you run a confessional, Bob Beer."

Walking away from him she turned and

added, ”When you get to Main Street, Mrs. Anne’s is to the left about a half mile. She’s had a ‘Room For Rent’ sign in her front window for two years. She will be glad to see you, and I’ll see you at the church at seven tomorrow morning. We’ll have a nice long discussion about Catholic Lutherans.”

Bob doffed his hat and bowed ceremoniously toward her while thinking to himself, “She could be trouble,” then he asked himself, “What are her pretty eyes up to? Where does she know me from? Perhaps, a sermon, somewhere”

Jeanette added, “Facilis descensus Averno,” which translates roughly as, ‘Easy is the descent into Hell.’

“Good gods,” he thought loudly in his head while smiling at her, “She understood every blessed word of my crazy blessing of the house.”

CHAPTER 9

Jeanette had been practicing snicker eradication since Jeffie's revelation. She had also become determined to maintain a more ladylike distance when conversing. Sitting alone in her kitchen the morning after the party, she snickerlessly listened to an imaginary breakfast companion, sipped a last bit of tea, said her goodbyes, and departed for her meeting with Bob Beer.

Jeanette's house was on School Street parallel to and three blocks west of Main. It was a five minute walk to the church, and she could see Bob Beer's horse grazing in the churchyard when she was crossing the bridge over Parish Creek. When she arrived she entered the church and found Mr. Beer standing in front of the Joan of Arc.

Without turning to face her he said, "This is a magnificent statue. Somewhat in the Greek style wouldn't you say, Miss Foudre?" He turned to face the Mary, and asked, "Did someone steal the baby?"

Jeanette, careful to maintain what she now considered a respectful distance, replied as Bob Beer turned to face her, "What could be in your nature that would allow you to consider that as a possible explanation? The fact is that the artist left Hanghat before he completed his work. . . . Have you seen the rest of the church?" As she spoke she successfully fought the innate urge to look away from his eyes and stare at his lips and chest.

"No," he replied, "I found the statuary here too interesting not to admire for a while, but please, if you would, show me the entire church. After the vestibule I can't wait to see the nave."

Jeanette noted a tinge of mockery in his last statement. She felt as though he had found the vestibule's statuary to be comical.

Bob was aware of how he had spoken, and had sensed its effect upon her, but he found himself to enjoy her company, and, like a schoolboy teasing a girl he had a crush on, he attempted to pique her with a second impertinent question, "Why did he have to leave town so fast?" But he had left himself vulnerable, and he had realized it as he spoke.

Without turning to face him, thinking she might in haste and temper stand to close to his face, a quirk which she, already feeling her pulse quicken, was particularly aware needed stifling. She replied, "You Mr. Beer should be capable of coming up with all kinds of reasons to depart rapidly . . . or should I say, abscond?"

Bob almost said, "Touche," but, instead, merely asked if she was ready to show him the rest of the church, all the while wondering how much she knew about him. Had she somehow seen the poster? But, then, he thought, "She wouldn't be here. Would she?"

Jeanette felt agitated, but the red color left her face as they began touring the building. Bob made no comment when he lifted a sheet covering the obviously provocative statue in the basement.

He lowered the sheet and thought about the Joan of Arc's full, pouting lips, then wondered about the prurient artist and what that artist considered his chisel to be.

Back in the nave Jeanette asked Bob to sit so they could talk. He sat down in the front pew. She seated herself in the pew across the aisle.

She began the conversation and very bluntly said, "I don't feel as though I can trust what you say, Mr. Beer. You see I have in my possession a wanted poster with your face on it."

He calmly and quickly replied, "Not a bad likeness is it? It was copied from pamphlets I carried. Pamphlets meant to introduce clients to my various services. The original was drawn in Dallas by a very exacting portrait artist—too exacting. It looked just like me."

Jeanette suspiciously yet politely asked, "And what would your various services be, Mr. Beer? Do you have your pamphlet with you?"

"No. I abandoned most of my meager possessions during a rather hasty exit from Heespud City."

"After the flimflam? After you were caught. . .or did they detain you?"

"No. I made what could be called a clean getaway."

"After you did what?"

"It's a long story. I should have to begin at the beginning for you to understand how the predicament leading to the poster came to pass. Would you listen to what I have to say?"

"Yes. I will hear your story. . . please

continue."

"It all began last year when I had my pamphlet printed. It seems the printer placed my likeness and name with the wrong text. The pamphlet with my picture read, 'Circuit Rider—Services in All Faiths. Donations Only.' My likeness and name were to go on a page listing my talents as a writer of family histories, biographies, news articles, and local histories and tales of local events.

I told the printer about the mistake, and his nephew, a Dallas County deputy sheriff who worked part time with his uncle, told me that I had made the mistake, and to pay up. Under coercion, I did just that. I reluctantly paid, grabbed the pamphlets and walked to the front door where I turned and faced the printer and his ill-tempered nephew, then I tossed the stack of pamphlets into the air. They fluttered onto the floor, and I, with a smile on my face and preparing my hand for a kind of salute, looked up to see the nephew pointing a pistol at me. I was forced to pick up the pamphlets, then he arrested me for vandalism and vagrancy.

A week later I rode out of Dallas with the pamphlets and not a nickel in my pocket. I was suddenly cast as a circuit rider out of necessity. I relied on my religious upbringing and knowledge of Latin, and, before long, my sermons were being well received. The resulting income was sufficient so that I began to save a little money toward becoming a writer again.

All was going smoothly until Heespud City.

There, where I was substituting for the Lutheran pastor who was out of town, I was called to the residence of one Mrs. Adelaide Schnorten. She appeared to be at Death's door when I arrived at her bedside. Soon I heard male voices coming up the stairs, and a maid entered the room and asked me to wait in the hall. Three men went into the bedroom and shut the door, leaving me and the tearful maid standing outside Mrs. Schnorten's bed chamber.

The maid went downstairs, then I heard one of the men with Mrs. Schnorten raise his voice in an assertive tone. Becoming concerned, I listened at the door and heard the men cajoling, then insisting that the dying woman sign a new will they were presenting to her.

I heard one say, "Just take the pen. I'll guide your hand."

The old lady refused and groaned that she wanted her money to go to her grandchildren and not to the city. I later found out that the men were the mayor, a crony of the mayor, and a distant relative of Adelaide Schnorten.

Then, the old lady let out a forlorn howling sound—then silence. I thought she had died, so I opened the door and saw one of the men grasping her hand and a pen, moving them over a piece of paper held by a second man.

The third man restrained me, saying, "She's not dead yet. She's not dead yet."

I could see, however, that her open eyes were not seeing anything. At that moment the maid and the doctor rushed in, and I brashly did something for an old woman and her grandchildren. I hurried to the man who was folding the will, with its forged signature still drying, and tore the document from his hand. I clutched it tightly, pushed the She's-not-dead-yet man out of my way, and thundered down the stairs to my horse.

I galloped to the outskirts of town where I paused to burn the document. Then I hid out in back country for a few weeks where, out of pressing necessity, I subsisted on pilfered chickens and corn; fully intending to someday compensate the unknowing donors.

Eventually I came upon one of the wanted posters attached to a tree. Until then I wasn't sure the wicked trio would have the nerve to charge me with anything, lest I bring their conspiracy to light.

And here I am, in lovely Hanghat; wanted for flimflam and repugnant behavior."

Jeanette had placed her elbows on the arm of the pew and shifted her position such that she had listened to the exciting story with her face cradled in her hands.

She still held that pose and was deep in thought when Bob said, "Your posture is almost the same as that of the second person listening to my account."

Jeanette straightened up and turned to look around the room, but saw no one.

"Forgive me, Miss Foudre, I'm speaking of the statue of the man kneeling at the prayer stool."

Jeanette stared at the rapt St. Thomas. Then, Mr. Beer's comment about the listening statue sparked an incredible idea—an idea inspired by a growing regard for Mr. Beer and the desire to have the church hold regular, Sunday services; hoping that a weekly dose of religion, with accompanying homiletic topics concerning fidelity, could be a way to reduce the uplift's rampant promiscuity.

Forgetting her new spatial behavior, she approached Mr. Beer, who had stood up. Standing twelve inches face to face, eyes to lips for a slight fraction of a second, then, eye to eye she spoke assertively, "You're not an ordained minister of any denomination, and you're certainly not a Catholic priest. Well then, I must more than suggest that in the Lutheran Catholic confessional a statue of St.Thomas alone listens to confessions."

Bob turned his head and looked at the statue and said, "St. Thomas the Doubter, the perfect saint to listen to sins of the faithful. I think the idea is keen, and, from the looks of it, I think he will just fit into the confessional."

The two met at the church during the week. In private discussions in the priest's office they agreed that Bob would stay on a while in the role as minister. Both agreed that the church could not represent itself as Catholic or Lutheran, or any established denomination, so they chose to call it the Catheran Church, which avoided possible problems including the one that would undoubtably arise when Uplifters told outsiders that they were Lutheran Catholics, or Catholic Lutherans. It was also agreed that Jeanette would from then on refer to Bob Beer as, Robert DeBiere.

That next Sunday during the first ever service in the Greater Uplift Catheran Church, Reverend DeBiere, at Jeanette's behest, delivered a homily about marital fidelity to an increasingly uneasy congregation.

CHAPTER 10

In 1894, Hanghat's Main Street business district consisted of the Hanghat General Store, the Fissile Wine Company, the Fissile Tasting Room, the Hanghat Feed and Grain, Cheval's Blacksmith Shop, Collage's Clothing and Fancies, the Agneau Bank, and Cadet's Barber Shop and Undertaking. The closest physician was fifteen miles away in Phleville.

A café called, Le Bistro, was the first business off Main Street, and it was built on an upwind, side street to escape the dust of Main Street traffic. In 1898 the Uplift Picayune would begin publishing a weekly newspaper, and the Bouquet Bakery would begin to mingle its fresh baked aroma with that of uplift's profuse wild flowers. It would be 1910 before any of the streets were paved. In that year five city blocks of Main were covered in red brick, but the side streets remained dirt until 1925 when they were asphalted for a distance of one block on either side of the red bricks of Main.

The streets parallel to Main were occupied by houses which were all built at acceptable distances from the outhouses behind Main Street businesses. It would be after septic systems were installed before the town wrapped around the corners of Main and built on the same blocks occupied by the original establishments.

Jeanette became one of the four teachers at Hanghat Public School when school restarted that last week in September 1894. Miss Fiona Pruclare was to be the new English teacher. She had come to town only in late August to add another member to the faculty, because Hanghat school was expected to have an enrollment of eighty-five students. Fiona boarded a few weeks at Anne's Room and Board, then she moved into a small frame house a few doors from Jeanette.

It was when Jeanette had Miss Fiona Pruclare over for tea the week before school commenced that she discovered that Fiona had taught manners in a previous position at a finishing school. Jeanette also found out that the older woman was rather brusque and formal, and severe in matters of etiquette.

Jeanette told the new English teacher how in need of the social graces were the children of the uplift, and then she expounded the particulars of the prevalent mannerisms to Fiona who squirmed in her chair and assumed facial expressions and performed head nods to signal her aversion to such behaviors. When Fiona arched or furrowed her brow, the bun of tightly knotted gray hair sitting on top of her head would perceptively move back and forth, but, luckily, the comical movement wasn't observed by Jeanette who could have suddenly needed to recall a joke she had recently been told.

At the moment she considered most opportune, Jeanette iterated the uncouth mannerisms, then quickly said, "Lessons in manners are what those children need. Dear Miss Pruclare, with your elegance and teaching expertise, do you think you would consider refining our student's manners once a week during the lunch period? If you have time, of course, to undertake such a challenging task as developing gentility in all our little Oliver Twists and Annie Oakleys."

Miss Pruclare warned, "Once a week would be insufficient to adequately effect changes in manners. No, it will take daily lessons to achieve permanent results. . . I know this from experience. Manners must be drilled and practiced."

During that school year, Miss Pruclare did achieve changes for the better in some of the student's dining behaviors, but it was in her English instruction that she was defeated totally, with the coup de gras coming after she had decided that the children would never understand any of Shakespeare's works. Upon that realization she had assigned her students the task of writing something about the Bard himself.

Miss Pruclare began reading a typical paper submitted by her students, "Shaking spears is not what he did because he was a writer who would of been better at spear fishing or war . . . ." That was all she could bring herself to read.

That paper marked the end of Miss Pruclare's year at Hanghat School, and the next year found her teaching elsewhere. She did, however, leave a lasting legacy that for several generations would determine the position of the pinky during the times any Uplifter held a tea cup. Miss Pruclare had drilled the students in the proper extension of the pinky finger. She would hold her fist in the air, and the children would do the same. Then on her command, "Spring your pinky on three. One, two, three," every pinky in the lunch room would spring out, and each child pretended to drink from a cup, while Miss Pruclare urged, "Keep those pinkies out. That's a sure sign of culture."

While Miss Pruclare was being taken to wit's end, Reverend DeBiere was living in the basement of the church while the town built a rectory next door. His series of homilies had resulted in having no limiting effect upon the uplift's yet overwhelming, extramarital mating drive, and consanguineous conceptions continued along at full tilt, but with a greater sense of underwhelming guilt.

Sexual liaisons were aided by the French tradition of hedgerows. Tryst secrecy was also served by honeyberry thickets which had grown from seeds brought by Overte Fissile from Louisiana and planted in her yard at Fissile House—as the Fissile home came to be called. The growing conditions on the uplift were ideal, and honeyberry seeds, spread mainly by birds, had grown into bushes in most parts of the area. On lower slopes, especially the sides of the uplift above the Bratity, the bushes grew to the size of small trees.

Lovers' trails crisscrossed the woodlands and thickets, and bowers in honeyberry bushes led to ground nests where couples fornicated quickly before straightening their clothes and exiting the dense tangles of bushes. Lone men and women were seen wandering through the underbrush of the uplift. Each carried a bucket or some implement which made them appear to be performing an agricultural chore or engaging in some other wholesome endeavor.

Conversation during Reverend DeBiere's encounters with these roaming fornicators led him to believe that nobody in the area could keep their milch cow in the fence, and that a few ripe honeyberries existed to be sought out even during the dead of winter.

Throughout the 1890's Hanghat had steadily grown in population, and Jeanette continued observing mannerisms and appearances. At night after grading students' work, she would work on the genealogical chart. She and Reverend DeBiere would socialize as guests at afternoon teas and parties, but she never saw him alone at the rectory or her house. The talk of the town became the question of when the two would marry.

During his first months at the church, the reverend had begun to suspect that the similarities among his flock had something to do with more than the water. He kept his suspicions to himself. He thought an answer might be found in a book about French society and behavior, so he mailed for and received books on those subjects. Finding no answers, he decided to ask for Jeanette's opinion on the matter. He thought, surely, what he suspected could not be going on. Families were stable and he was not aware of a single divorce or separation. He often wished he could be privy to the sins heard by the always rapt

St.Thomas, and once he had to admonish himself for pretending to dust close by the confessional during a confession by one of his major suspects—a woman with three children of whom only the oldest had black hair like the father. The other two looked different from each other, and different from the father, with one having blonde hair and the other, red. More evidence of something amiss was that only the oldest child could carry on a conversation without rambling among non sequiturs.

It was a Sunday in August of 1896, after church service, when the reverend found himself walking Jeanette to her door. He was surprised when she suggested he come in for a cup of tea.

"That would be delightful," he replied to her invitation. "I have been meaning to speak with you in the utmost confidence about a query suggested by certain features in members of the congregation. It often seems to me that they all could be related by blood—as if they were all first cousins, or closer."

Jeanette had always thought it would be someone from outside the uplift society who would broach the subject. She had wanted to confide in someone and discuss her conclusions suggested by her investigation of familial traits. Her trust in Bob Beer as Reverend DeBiere had grown, and she decided this was that time.

They entered the parlor, and she asked him to have a seat while she prepared tea. Soon, the Hanghat family tree, the one which Jeanette had stitched into a quilt, was spread out on the parlor floor.

"One side is the townsfolk and the other side is the rest of the uplift," she said. "I'll show you the Hanghat side first."

He saw a needlework tree. The trunk fanned out to become seventeen branches which were joined to each other at various heights. The needlework leaves in bright autumn colors, upon close inspection, were people's names stitched in script which formed the shapes of leaves.

She sipped her tea and said nothing while the reverend read. She suffered a twinge of apprehension because he seemed too interested. She thought back to his deportment since she had first met him. She recalled the 'wanted poster'. Was this the chance to do mischief he had been waiting for while pretending to be a caring pastor? Was he Bob Beer the chicken thief and flimflammer, or was he become Reverend DeBiere? "Is a beer in any other language still a beer?" she asked herself.

She was away in thought considering the possibility of a deceptively cunning Bob Beer, and was unconsciously, nervously snickering when she realized what she was doing, and abruptly ceased emitting the subtle noise. Returning her mind to the moment, she looked and saw a man made a stranger by her conjured apprehensions.

He turned his attention from the quilt and looked over at her. She wondered what his first words would be. Would she sense from those words that he had always been Bob Beer?

Reverend DeBiere asked, "What are you to

do? Surely this knowledge would ruin lives. No hint of your endeavor should ever escape. . . . And I must admit, Jeanette, how relieved I am to understand why you have been so insistent that I preach marital fidelity. I was beginning to feel that you were obsessed or that you were sensing a character flaw in me when you for the third Sunday in a row suggested that subject."

Her doubts were eased, "Oh, dear Robert, I should have told you sooner. After all, you have become a good minister. Will you forgive me?"

"Certainly and most assuredly dear Miss Foudre. Yours has been a burden in this matter. And don't worry. I'll preach marital fidelity as often as possible without seeming to be obsessed with the subject. I'll be subtle about it. . . use more parables, and, maybe, Canadian goose stories. You know, I had an acquaintance, an ornithologist, whose studies led him to believe that the Canadian goose is monogamous."

"Goose stories may impress the congregation, but don't forget the Puritans."

Robert quickly reminded Jeanette, "You're forgetting about Hawthorne's Scarlet Letter, and my being a minister, and all . . . well, I'd rather not mention the Puritans in this context."

"Then, stick to the goose analogy. . .I wonder if any other animals are monogamous?"

Late in the afternoon twilight the reverend walked back to the rectory. For the first time he noticed how many honeyberry bushes grew in patches around the town—patches big enough for two people to disappear into. Then, a block away he saw a man go into a honeyberry thicket. The reverend ducked behind a bush, waiting to see him return to view, but nothing happened until, in the early darkness, a woman emerged from the same place the man had disappeared. After an hour under a rising full moon no other party had emerged from the bushes, so the reverend began to casually walk toward the scene as if he were out for an evening stroll.

He glanced into the bushes and asked, “Is there anybody in there?” No reply.

He ducked into the opening and found only a neatly folded pile of men’s clothes. He strolled away toward the rectory thinking that, indeed, Jeanette did not know just how aberrant Hanghat had become in its isolation.

CHAPTER 11

Early in 1899, sometime in the spring of

that year, a traveling salesman found Hanghat—which was not easy to do because only the map of Heespud County suggested its existence. The salesman drove four white mules pulling a Conestoga wagon. He had been having no luck in the surrounding county seats at selling his most special product. With it and two cases of his fallback product remaining in his mule-drawn wagon, he had stumbled upon the cutoff to Hanghat from Tick County Road 4. He looked at his map of Texas and could not find any town between where he was and the Bratity river to the east. He sorely needed to get rid of the burdensome special product. On a salesman's hunch, and it being a Saturday, he turned the team of mules down the trail by the maildrop outhouse on which was nailed a sign reading, "Hanghat, Texas—3 miles."

He arrived in town and caused quite a commotion. People gathered and gawked while he stretched a banner from the wagon top to a pole he erected on the wagon's tongue. The banner read, "MARVEL TIME CAPSULES & ELIXIR." He placed an ostrich feather plume into the harness on top the head of each mule. After more people gathered, he delivered his pitch.

Three hours later he had sold a case of elixir and the time capsule, and he was departing Hanghat with forty more dollars, three cases of wine, and forty-eight jars of honeyberry preserves.

The time capsule was a cylindrical, enameled steel pot, two feet in diameter and eight feet high. It had a lid which, according to the

‘Lifetime Guarantee,’ would: “. . . keep the contents secure, pristine, and dry for 1000 years when properly fortified.”

The town began deciding what objects would go into the capsule, and for how long. Arguments led to formation of the Capsule Committee which then rejected the encapsulation of such things as a bee hive, a glass eye, a complete set of fingernail clippings, and a stuffed and mounted Spot, and not just any Spot, but the famous Wet Spot who had pulled a drowning child from the Bratity in 1897. The Capsule Committee rejected suggestions that the capsule be opened after one month; also rejecting one year, and a thousand years. Then by a vote of five to five, it was concluded that it would be opened in fifty years.

The reverend was asked to suggest an article for posterity. He consulted with Jeanette, and they decided to place the quilt into the capsule. It was a way to tell people about their real family ties at a time in the future when the knowledge would cause no despair and wreck no marriages and families. People will want to know their heritage, they told each other.

The two also vowed to deepen the gene pool by bringing people to the uplift—people from far away, or Tick County, if necessary. To do this they founded the Greater Hanghat Chamber of Commerce.

That December the fourth in the year of our Lord 1899, the hermetically sealed enamel pot containing its thousand-year certificate of guarantee, along with objects used in daily life, were placed inside a ten-foot cube of brown brick, capped by a thick slab of concrete. People had included letters addressed to future children and grandchildren. One letter complaining about having no service was addressed to any future postal carrier.

The quilt, rolled tightly around a letter explaining the information it carried, was wrapped in linen before others could get a good look at it. It was the last item placed into the capsule.

The rejected figure of Wet Spot was given a place of honor on a pedestal in a corner of city hall.

Another big event in 1899 was this announcement in the Uplift Picayune, "Mr. and Mrs. Sans Foudre announce the engagement of their daughter, Miss Jeanette Foudre, to Reverend Robert DeBiere." Three children followed their marriage in 1900—Thomas in 1901, Isidora in 1902, and Ethyl who was born in 1904.

After the birth of son, Thomas, Jeanette had come to wonder if it would be better for future children if, as a last resort, the Uplifters would continue mingling their genes, even if that meant extramarital sex with outsiders. After all, her husband had said that he was still seeing a goodly number of would-be, rogue cow milkers and winter honeyberry pickers; proving that his homilies were not succeeding. She didn't know that the inception for her new, iniquitous reasoning was created by her own subconscious urge to mate outside her marriage; an urge slowly emerging into her conscious thoughts and desires. Even though this profound alteration in her attitude had only come since the birth of her son, she did not consider that the gene-fomented desire that her conscious mind was attempting to suppress had been catalyzed by the birth of that first child.

She told herself that it would be better for all concerned if she persuaded her husband to abandon any mention of marital fidelity, and she told herself that it was of healthful benefit for posterity that Hanghatters should continue mating outside of their marriages. If so, a hitherto before unawakened personality reasoned, then she must also do her duty and mate with the first good looking and otherwise appropriately strange man that came to town.

While she was considering this new charge, she found herself walking around the neighborhood looking for honeyberry thickets which could hide two adults—one on all fours.

Jeanette perfected a solution for her new uncontrollable thoughts, but she never realized that the drive to mate outside marriage appeared in all the Sire's female offspring only after having a first child. Before the year was out, she would force herself to cease imagining the faces of handsome strangers, and she successfully, with the helping hand of assiduous self control, denied herself romps in a honeyberry thicket she had already selected. As it came to be, her three children were all fathered by her husband.

For the first year, or so, after the time capsule's installation, most people traveling on

Main between 2nd and 3rd Streets would take notice of the monument setting in the center of the otherwise vacant, city block. A small bronze plaque which simply read, "HANGHAT 1900 TILL 1950," mounted on the Main Street side, would someday make future Hanghatters think the monument was a tomb.

Eccrine Fissile died in 1903 at the age of seventy-nine. Overte, remaining in good health at the age of seventy-eight, held his wake in the Tasting Room where she and the other mourners toasted to his memory until she passed out drunk along with several others.

In1905 Overte commissioned a bronze work of art to be placed atop the time capsule monument. That grande dame of Hanghat had said the monument looked like an empty pedestal and needed something to make it appear more monumental.

A year later a bronze, two times life-size Spot stood alert and on point, almost inside a bronze honeyberry bush, which to some people, when the shadowing was just right, appeared to be a bent-over women in a hoop skirt. At the unveiling during the applause just after the bronze was exposed to view, four Spots simultaneously peed on each corner of the time capsule's brick encasement, as it also became a pedestal for a statue befitting Hanghat's strange character.

The land where the time capsule was located set three blocks north of the central business district in an area with no other structures. The business area grew south toward

9th Street, and the time capsule's island, bordered by Main and East Street and 2nd and 3rd streets, was maintained and mowed less and less as the years passed. Honeyberries and other bushes invaded the once well-kept lawn. Eventually, hackberry and oak trees grew uncut and by 1940 the monument and its contents, and the load of bronze on top, were out of sight and mostly forgotten.

So, Hanghat, Texas had miraculously come to be and had shimmied into the twentieth century where the wonders of modernity and gadgetry still awaited the time-suspended little town.

Reverend DeBiere's congregation had survived years of anti-fornication sermons. Toward the end of his long run of stories, he had run out of biblical characters and faithful, Canadian Goose couples, and had begun to include nursery rhyme characters. Many of the congregation's mothers of two or more children suspected that the reverend was speaking only to them as he explained how the old woman who lived in a shoe had acquired all those children.

CHAPTER 12

In 1908 De Bois Hardware and Lumber went into business in the first brick building in the business district. Hanghat's continued growth seemed assured, so other business owners felt it was time for them also to be in brick buildings.

A local artist, Guy Vin Gough, was sought after to paint Main Street as it would appear with brick buildings. The young artist, born in Hanghat in 1886, had to be tracked down because he lived in a warren of artists who occupied caves and tunnels in a labyrinthine growth of honeyberry bushes on a series of ledges leading eastward down to the Bratity River. He was selected for the "Soon-To-Be Downtown Area" painting because of the quality of his previous works, which included, "Wandering Albatross Sitting Upon Fissile House," "Wandering Albatross Sitting on Mr. Mouvoir's Head," and his groundbreaking work, "Wandering Albatross Sitting Atop Honeyberry Bush."

Guy Vin Gough needed the commission and reluctantly signed an agreement stating that he would paint no sitting wandering albatross into the "Soon-To-Be Downtown Area" painting.

That next noon he was seen sketching in front of his easel on the corner of Main and 7th. The business owners, pretending to admire his drawing, continuously monitored his work for an appearance of a sitting bird of any kind. At the end of a day of sketching, Guy took the canvas to the warren to color it in.

A week later the painting was unveiled at a ceremony in Fissile's Tasting Room. All present were pleased with the painting of an up-to-date, clean and bustling downtown of magnificent brick architecture, even though the artist referred to it as the "Wandering Albatross Sitting On A Cloud Over Downtown Hanghat." A small white fluffy cloud had been painted into the picture but apparently the bird was sitting on top of the cloud and out of sight.

Before the brick architectural remedy could begin, a fly had to be removed from the ointment. 1908 had become a wet year, and the crossing in the old riverbed was knee-deep in water and mud which bogged-down and stopped the first wagon loads of brick. It was time for a bridge.

Construction of a sturdy, one lane, wooden bridge was completed in three months on March 3, 1909. Rock and gravel were dumped and spread along the road to town, and the loads of bricks began to roll into Hanghat.

By 1911 all the business district was brick, except Le Bistro Café. The new buildings were topped with so many lightning rods that strangers probably wondered if the town had been subjected to some horrible accident, or if the inhabitants were merely paranoid. The wood siding which had been on the buildings was used to complete a city hall on West Street between 6th and 7th. The plan was to build a brick city hall as soon as funds were available.

During all of the painting and building and

bridging years, Jeanette DeBiere had quit her job as a teacher, and raised her children. Her husband continued preaching, and working in the general store.

Having a bridge was also meant to bring more people and economic growth to Hanghat. Among the first people to be attracted were three Heespud County officials. The word of the improved road reached the county seat only after the road was completed, so the county officials were peeved about not being consulted, and peeved about Tick County officials getting all the kickbacks from the construction materials. They were irate but they still had a plan for getting some money out of the deal. They had one problem—they were waiting for a new Ford Model T to arrive. That took until spring of 1910, by which time they had stacked penalties and interest onto what they figured was the county's cut on the action via a spanking new tax on illegally constructed roads and bridges in Heespud County since half the bridge—the two counties were divided along the center of the old riverbed—and all the new road winding its way up and onto the uplift were in Heespud County.

The dirt road to Hanghat joined the graveled but poorly maintained Tick County Road 4 midway along the inside of a decreasing radius curve that tilted in the wrong direction. The high side of the roadway was on the inside of the curve, making any vehicle moving faster than a horse and wagon tend to fly off the road. In civil engineering terms it would be called a decreasing radius, reverse cambered curve—a configuration to be avoided.

At the junction was a sign reading, "Hanghat– 3 miles," with an arrow drawn below the words. The sign was on a post, but since the high side of the road was on the inside of the decreasing radius curve, the top of the sign set beneath a passing driver's view. A passenger could catch a glimpse of it if they were looking that way, but, usually, they were too busy trying not to be thrown onto the driver of the vehicle as the decreasing radius built up the centrifugal force. The only people to successfully navigate the curve and make the turn on the first try were those who knew where it was. The result of all this was that very few people ever stumbled onto or went to investigate a town not shown on a Tick County, or a state map.

On April 1, 1910, the three Heespud County officials drove out of Heespud City in a new car. They had received a respectable amount of money from an unrespectable deal, and had stepped up from the Model T to a touring car with a powerful engine. They crossed the Bratity into Tick County and turned north. After a big lunch of fried catfish at a riverside café they drove to Tick County Road 4 and took a right.

After a stop to pee they were on the road again and approaching the decreasing radius, reverse cambered curve at showoff speed.

The front passenger caught sight of the sign to Hanghat at the last second and hollered, "Turn right!"

The rear of the large car slid to the left and the driver lost control as the car climbed the rising roadway to become airborne where the road dropped away from the wheels. It careened through the air rotating upside down before landing in a large, succulent and thick patch of poison oak. The overturned car was below the roadway and out of sight of passing traffic. Trapped in the car and surrounded by the poison oak was the right honorable mayor of Heespud City, a man known as Bullfrog Schultz, and the two main accomplices in his administration—the three men who had attempted to rob the grandchildren of the dead Mrs. Adelaide Schnorten. It took till sunup the following day for the three to break and twist their way through the poison oak to bare ground, and then dig themselves out and escape from the car.

They struggled up to the county road and stood there waiting for a ride to anywhere they could obtain calamine lotion and a shot of whiskey. In the two hours it took for a vehicle to pass, they had just about scratched off what remained of their tattered clothing. Finally, a horse-drawn wagon came by and gave them a slow ride into Phleville where they were arrested for indecent exposure.

It would be eleven years before any Heespud County officials attempted another journey to a town which Bullfrog, still scratching six months after the incident, had excluded from a new edition of the official county map, having decided that Tick County deserved the foul place and all the bastards who lived there.

CHAPTER 13

Jeanette was busy raising her three children and did not return to teaching until 1917. Robert still preached every Sunday and worked in the general store.

With the new brick commercial area, the businessmen of Hanghat decided that it was time to accelerate growth by bringing in new people and industry. Hanghat and the entire uplift had lived on original family wealth and agricultural income from the uplift farms, but most family fortunes had dwindled and agriculture wasn't doing well in 1911. The uplift's three minor products were holding their markets, but the entire economy could not be sustained by sells of ripe cheese, marmalades, and deluxe, hand sewn throw pillows made by denizens of the art warren.

Hanghat's business community took a new interest in the chamber of commerce founded by Jeanette and Reverend DeBiere. The organization had been dormant after its originators' attempts at attracting new people proved futile.

In 1912 a rejuvenated Greater Hanghat Chamber of Commerce began to send promotional letters to private industry and all levels of government. The letters mentioned that Hanghat, even though isolated, was only five miles from the end of a spur off a railroad line from Fort Worth.

It was then decided that the expected influx of industrialists would need a large sign at the cutoff to find their way. A sign was built and erected at the cutoff. It read, "HANGHAT–CITY OF THE FUTURE," with the customary red arrow pointing the way at the sign's bottom.

As soon as the Phleville Chamber of Commerce discovered its presence they demanded it be removed, arguing that no town in another county can erect municipal road signs in Tick County. The case ended up in a state court where the Hanghat sign was declared legal. At that point the Great Sign War of 1912 commenced.

Two days after the court decision the sign was found missing—just the posts remained. So, Hanghatters placed another sign, and it too went missing.

A third sign was erected and the Hanghatters lay in wait to discover the sign-removing culprits. In the middle of the night, sign-removing thugs arrived and went about their work. One of the Hanghatters had brought a shotgun loaded with rock salt, and he opened up on the sign removers before they could do any removing.

The next day the Hanghatters moved the sign twenty feet and set its posts in the middle of the infamous poison oak patch.

After that, the price for sign thugs was too high for their employers to pay, so in a new hit-and-run campaign the Phlevillains would drive by and shoot the sign with buckshot. Then, in 1913 after Texas Rangers arrested one fellow who was caught in the act, the incidents of vandalism became less frequent.

As it turned out, nobody replied to

Hanghat's promotional letters except a federal government agency which said it would keep Hanghat in its records of possible locations for a government project some day, if ever needed.

By 1915 the grand sign had been shot to hell and never repaired. The uplift continued in isolation. While the sign had been up, some traveling salesmen did visit. They found Hanghat a slow market for quantity, but discovered it was a good place to dump small lots of slow selling items and samples of gadgets that had never generated any orders.

Hanghat was quiet from the days of the sign war until 1919. Jeanette was the busiest person in town. For years she had sought new ways to design quizzes so that at least some of the more Sire-related students could successfully pass them, but her prodigious efforts were as yet being thwarted by students who, she was beginning to suspect, were idiot savants possessing a miraculous ability to answer rational test questions with compositions too obtuse for her to grade, or even comprehend.

One in ten residents in the United States had a phone by 1914, but in 1919 there was yet to be telephones in Hanghat. A telegraph line extended from Phleville, but Phlevillains tended to ignore sending any news to that much detested place they still considered as an out-of-county business rival. It was only after WWI was over that Hanghatters knew it had been fought. They had heard that a war was brewing, but for the year the United States was in it, Hanghat's telegraph line was down, and no outsiders visited.

On May 3, 1919, one Edward Dumas found the cutoff leading to Hanghat. He drove his Model T across the one lane bridge and chugged up the winding road to the top of the uplift.

Edward Dumas was twenty-four years old. One week ago he had departed his home in the Louisiana parish from which the founders of Hanghat had lived. He had come to the uplift to take possession of a farm which had been willed to him by his great-uncle who had died a bachelor. He had left his businesses, Dumas' Formal Wear & Live Bait and a fleet of seagoing fishing boats, under the supervision of his brother.

He stopped where the road leveled out, and he stood for a few minutes, looking at the view of the horizon toward the west and the land below the uplift. Then he started his Model T with its hand-crank, and continued along a flat road toward Hanghat. He admired well-kept fields, and after two more miles he came off the dusty gravel road and onto the red bricks of Main Street. He circled the business area, admiring the brick architecture and being amazed at how fast a dog with a large black spot must be, because every time he turned a corner, there the dog was. While touring and seeing what he believed must be the world's fastest dog, he nodded to townspeople sitting on curbs, chairs, hitching rails and wooden boxes. He was pleased to see that the local people enjoyed a good sit, because that made him feel like Hanghat wouldn't be so much different from his Louisiana hometown.

He came to a stop in front of the Tasting Room where the dog with the spot was suddenly asleep on the sidewalk by the entrance. Upon entering, Mr. Dumas heard a man behind a bar ask him what he was selling. He replied that he was not selling anything and offered no more information.

The man told him that, by the way, the Tasting Room was a wine saloon, not a tasting room, and that it was also serving shots of whiskey and a locally brewed ale.

After a glass of claret he asked the man about available rooms for rent. He departed with the directions to Anne's Boarding House—eight blocks up Main Street, and on the right between 13th and 14th.

After introducing himself to Anne Collage, the spinster sister of Jeffie's husband, Baptiste Collage, he paid two days in advance for just a room without the board.

After a bath and a rest, he strolled along Main Street, heading for the café he had noticed when first arriving in town.

Arriving at Le Bistro he discovered a young woman shutting the cafe's door. She asked him if he had come for supper, and he replied that he had.

"Good," she said, "You arrived just in time. I am the owner and I was just closing early, but I would be glad to prepare a meal for you. Please come in and sit anywhere."

He was impressed by her friendliness and how she had made a transition from appearing tired to being animated.

"My name is Joy," she told him.

While she cooked, she conversed with him from the kitchen. She told him how enjoyable his walk back to Anne's would be if he went along West Street, which was out the door and to the left. When she brought fresh flowers to his table she smiled broadly and repeated her suggestion for the path down West, and she mentioned how the springtime aromas of honeyberry bushes were best along that route.

As soon as she placed a dessert in front of him, she said, "I must leave now. If you would just close the door behind you and don't worry about locking it. You can put the money on the counter, or pay me tomorrow." She was out the door before he could reply.

Edward Dumas sat alone in Le Bistro. He wished that the beautiful and lively woman could have joined him for dessert. When he completed his supper, he placed payment for his meal on the table and went out the door, making sure it was securely shut. He stood on the wood walkway, patted his belly, and belched. Then he walked to the left toward West Street and the last gray-orange light in the early evening sky. The streets were vacant.

"Everybody must be sitting at home," he thought "Small towns go to bed early."

After two blocks, and while between 7th and 8th, a bush spoke to him. It beckoned to him, speaking low, almost whispering.

He paused by the bush and pushed a branch aside to reveal a naked female in light just sufficient to allow the perception of her dimensions and complexion.

"It is Joy. Come and take me."

She held her arms out to him. He entered the bush.

The next morning found Mr. Dumas down at Le Bistro for breakfast. He entered to find the café crowded. People nodded at him and indicated that they had heard a stranger was in town who was not a salesman.

A man wearing an apron approached him and said, "My name is Terry LeConte. It is a pleasure to meet you, Mr. Dumas. Anne Collage has spread word of your arrival. Your family and mine knew each other years ago in Louisiana. Come, meet my wife."

Mr. LeConte ushered him toward the kitchen where he saw Joy and a child, "This is my wife, Mrs. LeConte, and our son, Marshal."

Mr. Dumas, surprised and chagrined, nodded his head and nervously announced, "It's a pleasure, I mean it's pleasant to meet you, Mrs. LeConte."

Mr. LeConte added, "Joy is my wife's given name. . . and she is a joy."

"All the good for you, Mr. LeConte. A wife should be a joy to her husband and children," replied Edward.

Breakfast was followed by an hour of discussions and cigars. The Hanghatters were pleased to see someone from the old parish in Louisiana. Reverend DeBiere came in and invited Mr. Dumas to visit with him and his wife for morning tea at their home.

The reverend was giving directions to his house when Joy walked up and asked the men sitting at the table if anybody needed anything. She was pouring a cup of tea when the reverend said to Mr. Dumas, “When you pass 7th Street be sure to notice the large bushes in bloom. They are some of the sweetest honeyberry blossoms in town.”

“I have already discovered how wonderfully delightful that bush is, just last night,” said Mr. Dumas. “I took a stroll about town and was attracted to it. In the dark I thought it was a single bush.”

“After tea I would be pleased if you would allow me to accompany you to your new property,” said Reverend DeBiere.

Jeanette was pleased upon first hearing that new genetic material was coming to Hanghat. Then she heard that he was from the old parish and she began to worry about any connection the newcomer could have with Sire. She had been telling herself that the chances were slim, and how Sire, surely, had not been a busy-enough bee to make it to every flower.

Their guest arrived promptly for ten o’clock tea. Sitting in the parlor, Jeanette strained to detect any snickering. In attempts to evoke that evidence of family history, she was mirthful to the point of comedy, but Mr. Dumas laughed politely without a chortle or a guffaw, or the snicker. She asked questions which required extended answers from Mr. Dumas, then she listened, staring at his mouth to hear if he strung together any series of phrases that were arrayed among differing subjects. He seems coherent, she told herself.

When Jeanette went to the kitchen for more tea, Mr. Dumas leaned forward in his chair toward Reverend DeBiere and commented, “One can certainly see that your wife is a school teacher. And a most congenial one at that. I must say I feel like I’ve just been quizzed and don’t know if I passed or not.”

The reverend nodded his head in a circular motion which didn’t clearly convey its meaning, and stared at Mr. Dumas as if he were waiting for him to perform some feat.

That considerable and cryptic attention directed at Mr. Dumas had made him nervous; so nervous that upon Jeanette’s return with the tea pot, Mr. Dumas blurted out, “Too much tea can make one’s nervous auto won’t make it out to my great uncle’s at what time is it to be now.”

“Heavens to Betsy,” said Jeanette loudly. Then, disguising the reason for her surprising exclamation, she quickly added, “I didn’t have any idea I was keeping you, dear Mr. Dumas.”

Mr. Dumas was silent for a moment, then replied, speaking slowly and using short sentences which sounded rehearsed, “Yes it is late. Perhaps I’ll inspect the farm . . . tomorrow. I must return to my room now. Thank you so much for the tea . . . for the chat.”

The DeBieres watched Mr. Dumas drive toward Main.

“A new man in town and he’s a blood

relative to almost all the eligible ladies in town," decried Jeanette to her husband.

"Don't condemn him, Dear. Nothing in this matter is his fault."

"I know that it is no tragedy. . . just disappointing. I am so looking forward to the day a student can pass an essay test. When Mr. Dumas first came into the parlor, I imagined one of his children in my class making A's on the most difficult of essay questions. Just last week nine students in a class of fifteen scored a zero on a multiple choice test of forty questions. I didn't know how that was possible. It seems that one of them, even guessing, should have gotten a few marked correctly."

Her husband added, "Just think about it. It took a bit of work to reveal any of the characteristics that vex you so. Maybe you just flustered him with your questions. And, if you recall, he didn't come within two feet of either of us. I think that suggests that he is a very distant relative of whomever initiated all this, and may be only a great-nephew or a third cousin of some sort."

CHAPTER 14

The twentieth century was just beginning to arouse Hanghat in 1919. Only twenty, or so, autos and trucks were in town, as well as a few other modern contraptions that had made it onto the cutoff and up the incline.

An old McCormick reaper made the journey in 1919 to the farm of Terre Mouvoir II. That year, when his fields of grain were golden ripe, a large crowd of observers came to watch the big contraption on its maiden voyage across a field of wheat.

Farmer Mouvoir, with six pairs of reins in his hands, urged-on the team of twenty horses and mules hitched to the reaper. Then, with grinding and rattling and swooshing sounds, the machine began to move. The animals straining at their traces all had their ears back, listening nervously to the noisy thing following behind them. Farmer Mouvoir tipped his hat to the crowd of cheering spectators.

The mechanical marvel had made one cut along the edge of the wheat field when a sudden, very loud whirring sound started coming from the reaper's innards. This new sound was beyond what the apprehensive horses and mules could tolerate, and they went out of control. Before the animals ran themselves out, Farmer Mouvoir's prize reaper had cut wild swaths through wheat on the farm next door as the panicked animals turned and reeled in their attempts to escape from the menace following them.

The mob of animals, with the reaper still attached, came to a winded halt after they had run in one final large circle. Setting within the circle was a zigzag swath and a figure eight swath cut during the first frantic minutes of the runaway. During the fiasco the crowd of Hanghatters cheered and laughed until they were hoarse and falling off their chairs. Mr. Mouvoir, the inadvertent originator of crop circles, who had always maintained a stoic air of no nonsense and was never known for mirth, began to laugh so heartily that he fell from the reaper and rolled on the ground. Through with his fit of laughter, he turned toward the crowd which had scooted their chairs inside the crop circle and close to the infernal machine.

Farmer Mouvoir wiped tears from his eyes, removed the bandana from over his nose, sneezed a number of times, then said, "As soon as the animals get their wind back and forth, anybody that wants to a ride. . . well water is not dry, just jump on. It's a bed of roses better anything at carnival. I swear it was there when I left it."

An adventurous eight of the spectators who had understood his offer, jumped onto the reaper and, with chairs in hand, rode atop the reaper as it began the trip back to Farmer Mouvoir's own fields.

The reaper episode was typical of problems encountered by Uplifters and Hanghatters as technology crept into their lives—things seemed to get out of hand. The newfangledness that swept across America was slow in coming to Hanghat because the inbred Hanghatters felt uncomfortable when their routines were altered. The outbred Hanghatters would have been more new-fashioned, but they had been effectively cutoff from the rest of the world because of America's first oversized ranch-style home and a decreasing radius, reverse cambered curve.

The uplift was little altered by the clamor of the nineteen-teens, but Hanghatters were blown off their chairs by the Roaring Twenties—ten years which brought suffrage and Prohibition and electricity and radios and telephones.

The Hanghat Women's Suffrage Movement was led by the elderly Overte Fissile. Overte, who had turned ninety-five in 1920, worked from her library at Fissile House, and her army of suffragettes was led in demonstrations by Overte's daughter and field general, Eclaire Fissile. Being Hanghatters, they had not ever held a march down Main Street, but they had held tea and wine rallies at Fissile House and at the city hall, which had yet to be bricked.

Finally, the women possessed sufficient anger to actually abandon their well-seated, enclosed demonstrations and schedule a march from the south end of the bricked portion of Main, all the way to city hall—a distance of five-and-a-half city blocks.

At noon on October 3, 1920, the suffragettes began their march. In the front ranks were the movement's most ardent supporters including Jeanette DeBiere. Jeffie Foudre marched because Jeanette had given her no choice, but with Jeffie was her twenty-year-old activist daughter, Genevieve "Sunshine" Collage, who was impassioned about the demonstration and its goal.

Genevieve was the prettiest girl on the uplift. She had been a tomboy, but that behavior, having upset her great-grandmother, Overte, caused Genevieve's departure for an Eastern finishing school as soon as she turned eighteen.

At finishing school she had been a member of a rogue chapter of suffragettes. The school was finished with the wild succulent young woman before she could be 'finished.'

The school's headmistress had written to Overte: ". . . Genevieve is not responsive to matters of etiquette, is intellectually promiscuous, and she has on many occasions brought about lapses of eupepsia in all of her teachers."

Genevieve sparkled with blue eyes and light brown hair that would have been sun-streaked like it had been in her tomboy days, but now, to Overte's delight, she was never seen without her parasol, which she carried only because it made her family happy. Overte, Eclaire, and Jeffie were also pleased about the other improvements they saw in Genevieve. Since her return she was wearing dresses and keeping out of the sun, and the girl poured an excellent high tea . . . and, oh yes, the tenacious headmistress had succeeded in de-snickering the young lady and spacing her a respectable distance from whomever she engaged in conversation.

Jeanette counted 150 women in the march.

Several big drums kept a cadence and soon the parade sat as a crowd in front of city hall.

All the men and boys were told to be there for the speeches, or else. The women, after making the special effort of a walking demonstration, had more than requested the male's presence at the day's finale.

Jeanette stepped onto a speaker's platform and began her memorized speech, "Citizens of Hanghat, we women of Hanghat have long suffered inquietude about the matter of being denied the vote. Why is it that we are subject to follow rules set forth by elected officials, but we have no vote to determine who those officials are to be? It seems only fair and just that . . . ." Jeanette had ceased speaking because of the rising voices of the men speaking among themselves.

She glared at the men and said, "Gentlemen, if you please, I would like to continue."

The banker, Mr. Agneau, replied, "Just a moment Mrs. DeBiere. We men have just had a startling revelation brought about by your speech and the subject of the day. It seems we also have never voted."

It was true. No Hanghatter, male or female, had ever voted—the town had no mayor or council. The only city employee was a man with a wagon and shovel who kept the streets clean of manure. As for county and state and federal elections, there was nowhere to vote except in Heespud City, whose officials didn't consider Hanghat as part of the county. Hanghat had never been notified about any impending elections. No potential Hanghat voter was ever registered to vote.

With this sudden dawning, the men had become as upset as the suffragettes, and they began to chant, "We want to vote, too. We want to vote, too."

A man shouted, "Well, then, why isn't now as good a time as any to elect a mayor and city council. Every adult, man and woman, can vote right now."

The crowd, quickly turning into a vote-starved mob, suddenly was ready for a voting orgy.

Someone in the back yelled, "Who will run for mayor?"

Another voice shouted, "I'll second that."

The incited voters-to-be looked around, waiting for a leader to step forward or for someone to place a name in nomination. Nobody came forward. Nobody placed any names.

Just when the epidemic of vote hunger was peaking, Mr. Agneau mounted the speaker's platform and yelled above the din of voices, "Everybody come to order. Listen! Listen! If anybody wants the job of first mayor of Hanghat, would they please raise their hand now so we can, all of the men and women, vote."

Among the several people who were not paying attention to Mr. Agneau's dare was Brandy Mouvoir, the sister of Terre Mouvoir II of McCormick reaper fame. Brandy's mind was concerned with the welfare of the pies for the after speech festivities, because just as Mr. Agneau had begun speaking, she had spied two Spots entering city hall where the pies set on tables. So, unaware of the consequences, she raised her hand to say that two pie thieves had just entered city hall.

Brandy Mouvoir was mayor of Hanghat till Prohibition ended in 1933. Hers was an administration fondly remembered for its benign neglect of federal law and the installation of electric, street lamps along the bricked stretch of Main.

During Hanghat's first, universal suffrage election day, two people were trying not to be seen stealing glancing at each other—Edward Dumas from under his tilted fedora, and Sunshine Collage between the fringes rimming her red parasol.

In December of 1920 a crate arrived at the Hanghat General Store post office. It was addressed to Mrs. Maude Malheur. Hanghat's first telephone switchboard had arrived. Maude had applied for the job and was selected to be the operator for the Greater Hanghat Telephone Exchange.

The switchboard and accompanying stool were set in the Malheur's parlor and made ready for service by technicians who arrived a week later.

Almost immediately after that, telephone poles began appearing down all the streets in town. By March of 1921 there were seventy-four houses and businesses with phones. Every phone line could be traced to a pole at the Malheur house where the wires were bundled and stuck through a hole the phone company had cut in the wall behind the switchboard.

Mrs. Malheur's husband, Mr. Guy Malheur, had suffered accidents since early childhood. He walked with a limp, the middle finger on each hand had dissolved away from some kind of perennial infection, and various scars were on his face and body. He had been struck by lightning, and the first automobile to come to town had backed over his arm while he was on the ground looking up the tailpipe. He was employed by Cadet's Barber Shop & Undertaking in the undertaking division.

The childless couple had been married since 1910. Loneliness was the main reason Maude had taken the phone company job. Guy was often morose, but was affectionate to her. She liked people and she enjoyed conversation, so she had decided she would be happier if she had a job. She thought that telephone operator was the perfect job for her.

Each day telephone service in Hanghat began at six in the morning and ran till seven p.m. For the first weeks after phone service commenced, Maude would sit at the switchboard busily making connections and gabbing, but after the novelty was gone she found herself sitting for minutes without any ring ups. Thereafter, she used the idle time to work in her house and garden, and she perfected a three-ring dash from her garden to her switchboard. She must have been an athlete at heart because she had a goal of a two-ring dash from the yellow squash. When working in that far part of the garden, she wore light clothing and went barefoot for speed and rapid acceleration. The 110-pound woman who was built like a marathon runner became despondent after achieving a two-ring dash when she realized there was no way she could ever break that record. A one ring dash from the squash to the switchboard was impossible. She lost interest in customer service, and would mosey toward the ringing switchboard while saying, "Hold your horses, I'm coming."

Maude and Guy had wanted children since first married, but rare attempts at conception had been fruitless until Maude found herself to be pregnant only twelve weeks after setting her two-ring record. By 1928 she had birthed Marie, Luc, Guy Jr., Jean, John, Belle, Helene, Gigi, Leo, and lastly, Au Revoir—Marie and Au Revoir were the only children fathered by Guy Malheur.

Au Revoir had clung inside the womb for an extra month as if he knew bad luck awaited him on the outside. A midwife had to reach in and pull Au Revoir out. Years later while speaking about the disasters and accidents that were to befall the first and last born Malheur children, the midwife would say that upon his birth, Au Revoir had pulled himself along the umbilical chord, hand over hand, in an attempt to get back to the safety of his mother's womb.

Maude Malheur was the first Hanghatter to receive attention in a national magazine article that stated: ". . . So after having three separate births in seventeen months, Margaret Sanger's organization mailed a box of birth control devices and a short note of advice to Mrs. Malheur of Hanghat, Oklahoma."

Hanghat had experienced another misfire in its war for recognition. The chamber of commerce was furious. Oklahoma, indeed. A letter was written to the Governor of Texas, whose aide, a man from Tick County, tossed it in the waste bucket.

CHAPTER 15

Prohibition arrived in 1921 in the person of Tadpole Schultz. Tadpole had become boss of his father's political machine when Bullfrog choked to death on a quickly chewed and swallowed sheet of paper during a federal district court proceeding in 1918. Tadpole, not as politically adept as his father, had worked himself down to the position of federal revenue agent. Bullfrog's two cronies from the days of the Adelaide Schnorten affair had taken control over Heespud County where one was the mayor, and She's-not-dead-yet was the county sheriff.

Tadpole, to get revenge against the two usurpers, was actually enforcing prohibition in his district, and that included all of Heespud and Tick counties. He was raiding road-houses and seeking out stills in Tick County when he happened upon the cutoff to Hanghat.

"Who or what the hell is a Hanghat?" he asked his partner, Harley, as Tadpole stomped the brake pedal and turned the wheel hard right. The car came to a stop when it bottomed-out on the high side of the infamous curve. The two revenuers cautiously exited the teetering car, tilted their fedoras higher on their brows, and looked off the edge at a view of wrecked cars laying scattered upside down to the left of a bridge.

The junior agent, a tall thin man who always carried an axe while at work, declared, "Hell it's no wonder there's wrecks down there.

This damn curve is tilted in the wrong direction."

Tadpole looked behind him to see the road. "It's tilted down the other side. Why didn't those automobiles slide off the other side of this here curve? Answer that for me."

Harley replied, "It seems to be they were all doin' a right turn an' the way this edge drops down to that bridge, I reckon they flipped over."

Tadpole stared at the bridge, then said, "Where's that goddamn map, Harley? I Don't remember anything called Hanghat."

Harley reached into the car and pulled out the Tick County map. He was reading it when Tadpole jerked it from his hands.

"I didn't see any Hanghat . . . maybe it's somebody's darn name, Agent Tadpole. Maybe the Hanghats live across that bridge . . . why're you lookin' so glassy-eyed, Agent Tadpole?"

"Seems I remember something about Hanghat . . . my daddy mentioned the name . . . said he'd never been there and didn't ever plan on going. It must be a town."

The sound of tires in gravel made them turn and see Agent Tadpole's government car, with its brand-new red light on top, begin to roll down toward the pile of wrecks. The two watched as it gained speed and drove itself to the right, then onto the bridge, coming to a stop on the other side.

They arrived at the car and found it undented. "That's lucky," said Harley while kissing his axe, "That's pure-dee good luck."

"Good luck?" said Tadpole, "We almost lost my automobile. Good luck, hell. If that's good luck, why did I almost have a heart attack? Answer me that."

Tadpole got behind the wheel without looking underneath, and Harley went to the front of the car and prepared to turn the crank handle.

They drove up the rising gravel road, then, when almost at the top of the incline, Tadpole decided to shift gears, and missed. His automobile began to roll back down the incline because the trip through the wrecks had ripped loose the brake lines.

The car gained speed and Tadpole hollered, "Jump for it!"

The rotund Tadpole rolled to a stop, but Harley slid through the gravel on his face and axe. Harley, bloody, and Tadpole, dusty, got up and stood watching the car as it rolled down to where the road turned to the left.

This time the car didn't turn, and they watched it leave the road and travel down, out of sight. They waited to hear a crash, expecting the car to turn over or hit a tree or one of the boulders that set here and there, but they only heard birds and each other's breathing. They looked up the road toward Hanghat and saw nothing but countryside.

"Let's walk back to the county road," sighed Tadpole. "We'll see what happened to my new automobile. Maybe, if we can get to it, you can get our stuff out of it, then we can get a ride into Phleville."

Tadpole trudged and Harley shuffled through grass, following the tracks of the car and expecting to see it wrecked somewhere below. Tadpole whooped when they arrived at a lookout above the third place their straight-line path would cross the winding road.

Setting to the left of the other side of the bridge was the car. It had crossed the road in three places on its plunge down the hillside, and had acquired enough momentum to run across the dried mud of the old river bottom.

Harley, still with some blood and dirt in his eyes, could not see clearly. He asked, “Is that the automobile? What is that across that bridge?”

“It’s that goddamned Model T! It’s back on the other side. I can see the red light on top. That’s her alright.”

They walked the rest of the way on the road and started across the bridge. The car was setting as if it had exited the bridge and turned left before coming to a stop. Half way across the bridge they saw flat tires. At the car they found that the undercarriage was mostly missing and all four wheel rims were bent.

“That’s where it happened. Look,” said Harley as he pointed where faint tire tracks led across the dry riverbed and ended at a low rock ledge. “It made it all the way, except for hitting that ledge. Musta been goin’ like a bat outa hell when it hit. I wish it had’a had sense enough to cross the bridge again. Don’t you, Agent Tadpole?”

Agent Tadpole, carrying his new car’s red light, and Junior Agent Harley, still with his axe, stood beside Tick County Road 4 for two hours before a truck stopped and gave them a ride to Phleville.

Three days later an angry, Hanghat hating Agent Tadpole Schultz led a six-man, three-car raid on Hanghat—not sure what a Hanghat was until he arrived.

They screeched to a stop in front of the Tasting Room. They found no booze anywhere in town, departed, and never returned. Fissile Wine Company and the Tasting Room had run out of wine and everything else about two months before the raid.

It was during these hard sober times without French wines that a new beverage began to appear on the uplift. Honeyberries were discovered to ferment into a delicious mead-like brew, but with a delightful nose and complexity which, according to the uplift's alcohol deprived connoisseurs, was more than acceptable, since no Chardonnay was available.

By late that next summer all the honeyberries in the uplift had been picked and fermented.

Wandering fornicators found that their usual excuse much more plausible as more people, including non fornicators, wandered the uplift searching for unharvested bushes of the sweet little yellow berries.

A well-kept secret in the warren of artists was that their honeyberry bushes growing on the humid banks of the Bratity, bore upon them the noble rot—botrytis. In France in certain warm and humid regions the noble rot coats clusters of grapes like a powder, and lends a distinctive flavor to the wines of those climes. Growing upon the warren's honeyberry blossoms the fungi impregnated dimension and grace to yield a reflective je ne sais quoi in the resulting brew. The botrytis infection caused one in ten honeyberry blossoms to become marcescent, producing no berry, but becoming covered with thick layers of botrytis. These blossoms were the secret ingredient in the warren's most prized vintage brew, which they named Bourgeon, and, because of its limited supply, the inhabitants only drank it on special occasions like when a batch was fermented enough to give a buzz.

Like all secrets, this one, the Bourgeon, leaked out into the ears of Hanghat from the hands of one of the warren's resident artists who arrived, drunk and smelling of art and smoke, one noon at the Hanghat General Store. He had come to trade smuggled goods for tubes of oils and a roll of canvas. The artist known as Pewter, the older brother of Guy Vin Gough, set a quart jar of Bourgeon on the counter in front of Sans Foudre.

"I'd like to trade this for some paints and canvas," Pewter said. "A dozen tubes of oils and a roll of canvas."

"That's not something I can do. That's more than a jar of honeyberry brew is worth, even if there won't be much more around till next summer," replied Mr. Foudre.

"Just taste it," said Pewter as he reached into his bag and placed two more jars-full on the counter.

He twisted the lid off one and offered a drink to Mr. Foudre. "Here, old man, grab that wine glass off the shelf and pour this, then tell me if three jars are not worth a trade for paints and canvas."

Honeyberry brew deprived, Sans Foudre, not planning to make the trade as presented, but wanting a drink of brew, reached the shelf behind him and presented an ordinary wine glass for filling.

"No, no, not that glass," said Pewter. "This is no honeyberry brew ordinaire, this deserves to be sniffed and enjoyed. I'll only pour into that impitoyable . . . the one by the cigar box," he pointed at the glass. His finger swayed so that Sans could not see which size of impitoyable it pointed at. "This brew has the aroma of the underarms of Aphrodite," said Pewter who nodded yes when Mr. Foudre picked the correct size glass.

He poured an inch of brew, then while Mr. Foudre swirled the brew and experienced its aroma, Pewter did something drunks have been doing since Mesopotamia's ancestors first discovered brewing—his drunken brain attached itself to his vocal chords, which, allowing Pewter no time for thought of secrets or consequences, drunkenly vibrated, "This is the finest the warren makes, and there are plenty of berries yet to be picked this summer. Our berries have the noble rot, you know. Just like the grapes of Aquitaine."

On August 22, 1921, the warren fell, after its inhabitants had fought off pickers and pruners for two days. Pail carrying fornicators and non fornicators descended from the heights and picked every honeyberry and every withered and fresh honeyberry bud, and eventually, after finding the noble rot to also be coating the leaves, they plucked every honeyberry leaf.

The lush cover of bushes that shaded and secreted the caves and sheds and ritual spaces of the little art colony were denuded, and from across the Bratity and from the rim of the uplift, tables and hammocks could be seen among boulders and large rocks painted with faces of gnome-like creatures and portraits of various Warrentians. And scattered everywhere were more than a hundred chairs all of the same design, and all made by the inhabitants.

The unique wooden chairs were light but sturdy, had detachable rockers, elbow sockets on the arms, a lumbar-easing back, and could be described best by saying they were a design blend of Shaker and Buck Rogers. Guy Vin Gough, the chair's designer called it, the Mazette, because people, upon first sitting in one, would almost always comment, "My goodness this is comfortable."

The art colony, with its chairs, then relocated itself upriver to a grove of cottonwood and oak. There they dug in for the winter, but there were no flat areas—just a steep slope of tree-covered earth rising to the uplift. Life would be difficult away from the evergreen honeyberry bushes, under deciduous trees, exposed to the coming winter away from their totems; their paradise picked clean.

That spring after surviving a winter where the disconsolate art colony only produced two works of art—a painting of a broken and withered branch entitled "Fait Accompli," and a wood sculpture entitled "Those Demonic Ass Holes," which was a work of social commentary made from a six-foot tall length of tree trunk having many knotholes which were all painted various shades of purples and blues and reds, achieving a realistic hemorrhoidal effect.

The artists planned to return to their original site when the honeyberry bushes bloomed and leafed-out. As it came to be, however, the over-picked, weakened honeyberry bushes over the entire uplift, and down to the banks of the Bratity, succumbed to a blight of less-than-noble rot.

A diaspora was about to begin when Guy Vin Gough stepped forth to lead the little group of thirty artists to a place in the wilderness they could call home. After wandering for twenty hours they settled in a hollow by a white oak close to a creek with a rapid whirlpool by a red cave just to the south of Fissile House and less than a half mile east of Main Street. That summer they planted leeks and performed art in a honeyberry-less world.

It was Overte Fissile who, at the suggestion, then entreaty, by Sunshine, came to the rescue of the misplaced art colony which she concluded was a victim of Prohibition as much as anybody. Overte visited the artists and explained to them that they were now located on a part of her estate, and then she told them that she was deeding the place they had camped, a parcel of four acres, to a trust which would allow a productive art colony the perpetual right to occupy that property as an artists' sanctuary with a yearly stipend for the support of the group, in return for 25 original works of art each year.

A thick rock wall twelve feet high was constructed around the four acres to give the artists privacy and to give it what Overte referred to as, "That sanctuary look." Above a main gate on an arch she had the words, "In Memoriam Eccrine Fissile. Ars Longa, Vita Brevis."

Sunshine enjoyed the company of the artists, and, while the wall was under construction, she spent the days in the company of Guy Vin Gough whom she admired for his art and friendship. She had reverted to her tomboy ways and would appear on horseback wearing riding pants, a long-sleeved shirt, and a fedora with a brightly colored trailing scarf wrapped around it as the only insignia of femaleness other than her very beautiful face, engaging smile, and colorful parasol.

Edward Dumas also visited the art colony during those days of wall building. Sunshine would often find Edward and Guy together when she arrived, and the three would sometimes picnic together.

Wall construction continued and the art colony settled into creating art. Edward and Sunshine came less often, and then, not at all. Edward was soon seen courting Sunshine who was again, and more revealingly than ever, dressed a la flapper, or in latest, east coast fashions, wearing very feminine attire, as if making up those lost tomboy years when, for certain boys and young men, she wished she would have on occasion dressed more femininely.

Genevieve Sunshine Collage became Mrs. Edward Dumas on October 23, 1922. The couple honeymooned in Paris and returned to Hanghat in February of 1923 with Sunshine two months enceinte, with the baby already named by Sunshine as either, Heathcliff, or Edna. The child was born and named Edna Mae Dumas, who was destined to become one of the memorable characters in a town of characters.

Erlene Louise followed her sister, Edna Mae, into the world in 1924, then Betty Joe was born in 1926.

In the center of the sanctuary Guy Vin Gough, reclusive after the Dumas wedding, had drifted into wistful melancholy, followed by dejection, followed by abject forlornness. With some effort as well as circumstances—the loss of the warren followed by the loss of someone he had tricked himself into believing was a soul mate—he had finally ridded himself of a gnawing happiness that had prevented his expressing upon canvas a creativity he knew was trapped within his contentment.

The albatross sitting on his frontal lobe flew out of his mind, leaving an egg behind in the exquisite gloominess of his elating despair. When it hatched, the world he had never seen but knew existed, flew from the egg to reveal the things of the universe as they were seen by a rock or any clump of non gray matter. Guy Vin Gough was both in and out of a silver-lined Klein bottle of despair, and he was plummeting up to a surge of achievement he had longed for but been too goddamned consoled to see.

With his mind now free to access his grand and colorful vistas of exquisite somethinglessness, he was ready to begin painting. While fomenting, he added a stylish, La Boheme-like, robin's egg blue garret, with northern light, naturally, to the cottage he had built in 1923 just after the wall was completed. There he painted pictures of things and spaces that would have existed if the world had come into being without geometrical figures or organic growth.

His fellow artists empathized with his creative frenzy and left him in solitude, listening as he cried and laughed, throwing him crusts of bread and a returnable bota filled with wine (typical, mad artist fare) through the east facing, pie-slice shaped window of his atelier.

He painted in the garret until his disappearance in 1925 at the age of thirty-nine. He had left behind forty paintings and his twelve personal mazettes, which were payment for his three years at the art sanctuary.

The collection was taken to Fissile House where the paintings were set leaning against the walls and furniture of the library. At a public viewing, Hanghatters, sitting in the mazettes and drinking homemade peach wine, commented about what they didn't see in the paintings and asked questions of each other as if they were the only ones missing a point.

"What do you think?"

"My goodness, this is a comfortable chair."

"This painting doesn't look like anything?"

Pointing, "Neither does that one."

"I fail to see any redeeming connotation or semblance of anything."

"Can anybody see something in any of these? An animal, a tree, a pile of something? Anything?"

The onlookers turned to Overte for some kind of simile or metaphor that would successfully describe a painting or a part of a painting.

Overte calmly said, "It's like they don't exist . . . each one is a painting of nonthings."

It was non existentialism, an entirely new way of seeing something ex nihil, but all anybody that afternoon in the Fissile House library could see was that Guy Vin Gogh had achieved nothing, except a most comfortable chair.

The paintings, seeming of little value or quality, were not hung in Fissile House, but were wrapped and stored in the large attic and quickly forgotten. The mazettes, with rockers snapped into place, were set on the front porch and in the sun room.

Overte Fissile died in 1926 unbeknown to the world that she had for the last three months of life been the 1,264th oldest person on earth. Her estate including the art sanctuary was placed in a trust for the heirs, and was to be maintained by a trust fund of almost a million dollars. Her will stated emphatically that if any device ever replaced manual adding machines, then, invest the entire fortune in that invention—she had badly mangled her finger in the adding machine at Fissile Wine Company. The result of the injury was that the ring finger of her right hand was in the shape of a corkscrew. It had come in handy in the family business, but the finger had made her self-conscious. She had spent her life always trying to keep the finger out of view. On her headstone was written, "Je peux pas supporter ces pupains de calculatrices," which translates something like, "I hate damned adding machines."

Sans Foudre and Eclaire Fissile Foudre moved into Fissile House. They were in their seventies and both would depart this world after a few years of life in the grand mansion.

The mansion was then to be occupied by the Collages—Baptiste and Jeffie.

Edward Dumas had sold his holdings in Louisiana and built a house for Sunshine and the children southeast of town on a rocky point overlooking the Bratity.

Sunshine may have at times demonstrated mild twit-like behavior, but it was hidden from others, including her admiring husband, by her zestful joie de vivre and sexy looks. Sunshine's mother, however, with a giddy, annoying enthusiasm and too much makeup, could not hide to any degree the fact that she had become more twit-like as the years had progressed. Jeffie continued the Fissile House tradition of two galas per year, and the events would have been dreaded by the guests if it had not been for the attendance of the gracious and shining Sunshine Collage and a good sit in a mazette.

As for Jeffie's frequent candlelight dinners, prospective invitees would hide like quarry unless Maude Malheur had put out the word over the telephone that Sunshine would be present to ameliorate the affectations of her mother, for whom the title of Grande Dame of Hanghat had gone to her head.

By the end of the roaring decade nearly all the homes on the uplift enjoyed electricity. In most houses a light globe dangled from a chord in the middle of every room, and there was at least one wall outlet in each room, except the bath and the kitchen, because no one used a radio or phonograph in those rooms. The amazing decade came to an end after Hanghatters had heard hundreds of radio episodes of soap operas and nightly news which, after traveling as gossip from person to person speaking in discordant streams of consciousness, could appear as tales of how two guys named Sacco and Vanzetti had flown solo across the Atlantic and Charles Lindbergh had been executed. The most interesting effect of radio was that it caused the young people of the uplift to rapidly begin to lose what remained of their Frenchness. In 1930 the Americanized teens of the uplift exclaimed few "Sacre bleus" and "Mon Dieus," but more than four thousand "Holy cows."

CHAPTER 16

The advertisement in a Dallas newspaper read, "Seeking doctor of medicine. Newly built office (furnished) and a free residence (furnished) await the right man. About 2400 people to be served in area includes 800 townsfolk. Reply to: Greater Hanghat Chamber of Commerce, Hanghat, Texas, Care of Post Office, Phleville, Texas."

The year 1930 had been difficult for Dr. Leander Bertram. Thirty-two-year-old Dr. Bertram had set up his first practice in downtown Dallas, but, having come from a small town to attend college and medical school, a big city where a certain young woman could avert the passionate and devoted love of a doctor and become engaged to that doctor's idiot attorney friend did not appeal to him. Nowhere is where he had found himself wanting to be, and, after reading Hanghat's advertisement, and then searching without success for Hanghat on maps of Texas and at the public library, he came to the conclusion that Hanghat was that "nowhere" where he needed to be.

He departed Dallas in his green Oldsmobile pulling a trailer packed high with all his worldly possessions it could carry. He headed south with a map marked with a route to Phleville. His black bag was at his side, and his spotless Irish sitter, Hero, stood in the back seat with her ears flapping in the breeze.

He arrived in Phleville late in the day and stayed the night in the Bane Hotel, where the desk clerk gave him directions to Hanghat.

The next morning found him on Tick County Road 4 driving back and forth around a curve which fit the description of the curve the desk clerk had described; commenting on its danger and warning him to take it slow and to keep his eyes on the road. He could see the ridge and the winding road climbing it, just like the Phlevillain had described, but there seemed to be no road going toward it, and no sign and arrow. Then, on one of his trips through the curve, he drove up to the high side of the road and over the crown of the shoulder. From there, he could see down to the bridge and the outhouse-like shed with the sign and arrow.

On July 3 of 1930 the Uplifters had a permanent doctor for the first time. Dr. Bertram drove under a "Welcome Doctor" banner stretched over Main. He was escorted to his free residence on the corner of 8th and Side streets where he received help unloading the trailer. He carried his black bag across Side Street to his new office—a white, frame structure with green shutters and a narrow porch running across the front.

That afternoon after dinner at Le Bistro with local dignitaries, he was sitting in his own rocking chair, smoking his favorite English briar pipe on the porch of his new office with his trusty dog at his feet, and being stared at by two dogs, each with a great black spot on its side.

On the following day Dr. Leander Bertram treated thirty firecracker injuries which included sewing up the forehead of nine years old Marie

Malheur who had struck a tree branch while gaining distance from a lighted firecracker. In her dash to safety she had run over her two-year-old brother, Au Revoir, knocked him down, giving him a concussion.

Dr. Bertram had insisted on keeping the stunned toddler overnight for observation in one of the office's two hospital-like bedrooms, however, the Malheurs assured him that the two children were always concussed or otherwise injured, and they would just take them both home. Dr. Bertram was to learn that he would be treating Marie and Au Revoir and their middle-fingerless father for an endless variety of injuries from the bizarre to the classics, including slipping on a banana peel and stepping on an upturned hoe.

Not only was a physician in Hanghat, but new businesses also began building in 1930. In 1931 the Medico Drug store opened at Main and 8th, and Woolworth's 5 & 10 opened in a new building on Main, on the same block as Hanghat General Store. Soon the Shoe, Boot, & Leather Repair was occupying what had been a space between the general store and the 5 & 10. Collage's Clothing & Fancies was enlarged and renamed as Collage's Department Store. Cheval Blacksmith moved its one gas pump and holding tank to Cheval's Standard Service Station, built at the corner of Main and 10th after a service station located in the business district of Phleville exploded and burned down half of the businesses on Phleville's Main Street.

Signs were placed to tell those who would

still arrive on horseback or in a wagon that Main Street had become a “Horse-free Zone” and instructed horse people to park on a side street off the pavement.

To the chamber of commerce it seemed Hanghat was on the verge of growing like a weed, then the depression, the Great Depression, deepened. In meetings of their newly formed Hanghat Optimist Club, the businessmen assured themselves that expected growth would only be delayed for a short time.

The Uplift Picayune for the first time began to publish news of the outside world in the summer of 1932, because the editor had become interested in politics and wanted FDR elected president so he would not suffer reelection of Hoover.

Hanghatters sent a delegation to Heespud City and, after some legal filings by an Austin attorney they employed, Hanghat became a separate voting precinct which included the entire uplift.

In the presidential election of November 1932, FDR received 95 percent of the uplift votes cast by women and men. The ladies, led by Mrs. Genevieve Dumas, wore their old suffragette marching dresses complete with sashes reading, “The Time Has Come.”

Jeanette was still teaching in 1932. Her three children had graduated from Texas colleges and were living in California. They had not understood why their mother had insisted upon their living far away from the uplift. Son,

Thomas, was teaching, and Isadora and Ethyl worked in the motion picture industry. Jeanette was sixty and tiring of attempts to bring new blood into the uplift population. It had been thirty years since she and Reverend DeBiere had begun scheming, cajoling, preaching to remove Sire's legacy of inbred idiosyncracies.

But the legacy did not only produce twits. Some of Sire's offspring possessing above average intellect, but cursed by an inability to collate thoughts to speech, would sometimes inadvertently say something profound. Such was the case during a 1933 school debate between Phleville High School and Hanghat High when a Hanghat student stated, ". . . so we would not have time if everything was in the same place. With the little hand on the big hand there would be no space to move and, therefore, no time. Time needs space to march, or there would be no march of time" Years later, a similar statement would be the basic principle of the "Little Bang" theory of dimension closure, otherwise known as "Uncreation."

The promiscuity driven FL descendants' needed a new excuse for wandering about a honeyberry-less countryside in the post-blight milieu. They couldn't all be searching for a loose milch cow, so they spread the word about an ongoing search for a honeyberry bush that had survived the blight of '22. Rumor was that one bush had been discovered by a drunken Terry LeConte while out searching for truffles, but he couldn't recall where.

It was just before the 1933 school year was to begin. Jeanette was in her school room behind her desk when the principal came in escorting two, big-boned sturdy women followed by twelve boys of similar stature, ranging in age from sixteen to seven.

"Mrs. Koczlesky and Mrs. Kosciuszko—I do hope I'm saying your names correctly. May I introduce our science and Latin teacher, Mrs. Jeanette DeBiere. Mrs. DeBiere, these are these lady's fine young sons. They will all be enrolled at our school. Their families just bought the Mouvoir farm and the Trudeau farm, adjacent to it." The principal beamed as he spoke.

"It's my pleasure," replied Jeanette.

While she chatted with the mothers she could not suspend the thoughts racing in her; thinking shamelessly that here was a partial answer to the redundancy of the uplift's genetic material.

The principal had asked the boys something, but Jeanette only heard mumbling. She was awash in emotion after thirty years of seeking genetic salvation, and there standing before her was a line of future husbands all totally unrelated to any Uplifter. Then, she thought of the coming opportunity to teach a class capable of penning coherent answers to her foot-high stack of brilliantly worded but as yet virgin, unasked, essay questions.

The mothers were introducing the sons; each boy making a faint gesture of bowing as his name was called. Jeanette stared at the boys, not hearing a word, only seeing carnal salvation from a twit-filled future, and seeing a perfect score, a red 100, at the top of a page of coherently composed essay answers.

The group was leaving her classroom when she partly regained cognizance and shouted, "Good bye Mrs. New People and your lovely man-children."

The principal, after being in Hanghat for a year, was accustomed to unusual behavior and strange wordings, but he turned back into the room and informed Mrs. DeBiere that she may have fostered a rude impression upon Mrs. and Mrs. What's Their Names.

His next stop with the families was Coach Corbiere's office in the gym. Upon telling the coach that the strapping lads standing in front of him would be attending the school, the principal saw Coach Corbiere began to behave more strangely than had Mrs. DeBiere.

Coach Corbiere was not looking at new students. He was looking at the stars of an unbeatable football team. He only distantly heard the boy's names as their mothers introduced them; his mind was busy manufacturing gridiron fantasies of runaway trouncings of every team in the district.

After the introductions Mrs. Koczlesky said, "All our boys are crazy about football."

After Mrs. Koczlesky said those words, tears appeared in the corners of the coach's eyes. His Hanghat High Hedgehogs had never won a football game. Coach Corbiere's record was zero wins and twenty-four losses—four of them to that arch Phlevillain, Coach Sneerty, of the Phleville High Jumpers. The PHJ fight song ran through Coach Corbiere's mind, taunting him, "PHJ whoopty-do, we'll jump all over you."

The families were leaving when the principal told the coach, "I'll need to see you and Mrs. DeBiere in my office as soon as possible. Neither of you gave even an impression of concern, nor even appeared to be paying attention while I presented those ladies and their sons."

Coach Corbiere had prayed often for a miracle like this, and he had prayed hardest when the opponent's score went into triple digits. In those darkest times he had envisioned thick-necked angels arriving from heaven, and now he had his football team-to-be. He recalled their cherub-like, pinkish faces and imagined angel wings behind the boys. He saw them soaring above opposing linemen, passing and running at will. Sitting in his chair with his feet on the desk, he shut his eyes to see the closing of a cheaply bound old testament titled, "Hanghat High Hedgehogs–The Dismal Years," and the opening to the first page of a patent leather covered new testament. The title page read, "The Illustrious Career Of Coach Corbiere."

In the afternoon he went to confessional and told St. Thomas about his avaricious thoughts. He asked forgiveness, then asked Saint Thomas to let him beat the hell out of Phleville every time his team played them.

Prohibition ended in December 1933, and that welcomed first shipment of French wines arrived at the Fissile Wine Co. in February of 1934. Americanization had metamorphosed all but the Uplifter's love for Bordeaux's reds and whites.

After the end of the "Almost Happy Time," as the days of honeyberry brew were called, the populace was drinking various home brews and distillates of fermented peaches, potatoes, pears, or whatever was available. They recalled the winter they ran out of everything but fermented, mare's milk (kumiss). That period was remembered as the "Unhappy Happy Time." Many still retained the sour and fetid aftertaste of the kumiss, and they had decided that the only way to rid themselves of it was to swish a fine Bordeaux around their taste buds to wash away the tenaciously enduring humors.

The Tasting Room was crowded all that first day of the wine's return, and with ripe cheeses and perfect wine, the bad memories of Prohibition had become the kind of bad dream that was remembered upon awakening, but forgotten by breakfast.

Now for a discussion of the effects upon the Uplifters by the Sexual Revolution in America during the Twenties and Thirties. There was no effect—the Uplifters had already long ago revolted.

As for The Great Depression, it had little negative effect on the uplift economy which pretty much was self-sufficient—a kind of mini autarky.

Farmers sold or traded their products to each other, the downtown businesses traded and sold goods to each other, and money tended to circulate on the uplift with few dollars flying off to the lowlands. The businessmen were satisfied with thinking that if it had not been for the stranglehold of the depression, then, by 1938 the uplift would have been bustling with trolleys and crowds of shoppers.

A business going great in the country during those years of hardship was the movies, and early in 1938 a man came to town and bought the vacant lot on the southeast corner of Main and 5th, and the lot behind it. As soon as the deal was completed, the man left town.

One month later a construction company showed up, then, seven weeks later, Hanghat had a movie house with a marquee above a marble ticket booth with glass on three sides. An upholstered stool set inside the ticket booth. On the tower of the marquee was the name of the movie house written vertically— "Josephine Theatre."

From the outside it appeared like a theater ready and opened for business, but inside there were no seats or projectors—just an empty auditorium with a sloping floor and a movie screen at the low end.

The builders went away and the lonely looking Josephine Theatre set there neglected until 1939 when a truck of men with ladders arrived and put words on the marquee. The letters read, "Gone With The Wind—Coming Soon."

The letters were placed on the marquee

while one of the men searched through dozens of keys, trying to find the one which would open the entry door to the theater. Finally, he shouted, "Eureka," and went into the theater and out again.

"There's no goddamned chairs or concession or projectors in this damn thing," he told the men who were up the ladders placing the last letters in place. They all scratched their heads.

The men had a huddled discussion, then loaded their ladders and set up a camera across the street and pointed it at the theater. One man carrying a roll of electric chord went into the general store, and then he came out and laid the chord from the store to the theater. After some connections the hundred lights on the marquee began flashing light which looked like it was circling around and up and down the entire marquee.

Among the awed crowd watching the goings-on was Mrs. Genevieve Sunshine Dumas and her three daughters, Edna and Erlene and Betty Joe, who had been sitting and shopping.

One of the men approached Sunshine and asked her if she would sit in the ticket booth while they took photographs of the building. Then, with an obliging Sunshine smiling in the ticket booth, sitting on the upholstered stool, the movie men made some photos from across the street and, then, up close to the booth. Then they packed up and left while the crowd gathered around Sunshine asking her how was it to sit on the upholstered stool. Probably every person there wanted to enter that ticket booth to have a sit on a movie stool.

Sunshine said, “It was a comfortable sit, but I don’t think they locked the booth door after I left it. Maybe everybody can have a sit on the movie stool.”

Every face turned to look at the booth. Evelyn Baraque was first to the door. She sat on the upholstered movie stool until her brother pulled her off of it and sat down. Within an hour the word had spread, and a long line of Hanghatters waited their turn to sit in the movie stool. That evening an electric chord was run to the theater to relight the marquee. People would sit on the movie stool, then get up and return to the end of the line to wait for another sit.

The marquee lights ran and circled, the waiting line was noisy and animated, a car passed and a woman in it commented to her husband, “It looks like that movie house is open. Let’s go see the movie this weekend.”

The year 1939 came and went, but “Gone With The Wind” never did, and the Josephine never opened. “Gone With The Wind,” through the coming years, would shed a letter occasionally, and on Friday, December 5, 1941, the day of the district championship football game between the Haygap Balers and Hanghat High Hedgehogs, the marquee read, “Gone With The Win,” as the school bus carrying Coach Corbiere and his undefeated team passed the marquee. The coach saw the sign and knew that thick-necked angels had removed the ‘d’ to let him know that the game was in the bag, and that he, with a district championship under his belt, would be offered a coaching job at a big city high school and be gone with the win.

The Hedgehogs lost the game, and it was the Haygap coach who was on his way to the big-time in a town with over 5000 people. Coach Corbiere thought that he had mistakenly considered the pronouncement of the marquee to be about him. He told the story about the prediction made by the marquee and people began to watch the sign for any change which would have meaning. Those changes would occur, but like the Oracle at Delphi, the meanings would never be clear, but only riddles to be solved.

CHAPTER 17

Edward Dumas had often traveled abroad with Sunshine and their three daughters. Edward felt that travel was especially enlightening for children, so as soon as the youngest, Betty Joe, was six years old, the family departed for England and France. They were abroad for most of the time, coming and going until unsettled conditions in Europe led him to believe war could break out and leave them marooned on the Continent. Returning from Italy and north Africa in 1936, he decided to place the girls in public school in Hanghat. Sunshine had also mentioned that she would like to be at home for a while, so they settled into life in their fine house overlooking the Bratity.

People who had been suffering through Sunshine-less get-togethers at Fissile House were glad to have her return to stay. Jeffie had grown despondent as guests had become more difficult to garner, but she was instantly enlivened by a good turnout at the welcoming party she held for her daughter's return.

War came to Europe. Unlike WWI, the war had an effect upon the uplift. Voting in the presidential election of 1932 had placed Hanghat on the county map and created a voting precinct. That paper trail led the local draft board to send letters to every address in the uplift notifying residents that all men between certain ages must register for the draft.

A first bus load of draftees left Hanghat in May of 1942. The bus drove past a cheering and crying crowd then under a banner reading, “We’re All Behind You!” then past the marquee with its remaining letters reading, “one With The Win.” Some said the oracle meant that they would all be one in victory, others thought it meant that they would lose one of their sons to the war, and some fearful mothers saw it as meaning that only one son would survive.

Of the 123 men who eventually went for physicals, only fifty were drafted; the other seventy-three didn’t make it past the army psychiatrists. Of the fifty drafted, nine were killed in combat, jealous husbands caught twelve fornicating in haystacks, eleven returned unscathed, and eighteen returned with war brides. This latter state of affairs satisfied Jeanette and Robert DeBiere because they saw it as another dilution of Sire’s twit-filled bloodline.

Like most small towns in America, Hanghat should have laid dormant for the duration of the war—but the town was part of the uplift, where something dynamic seemed to happen almost as often as the lightning storms the plateau was famous for.

The primordial extra special urge to reproduce during times the species’ survival is threatened brought about an over abundance of wandering fornicators, many of whom no longer even carried pails to disguise their lustful intent.

Many of the younger men and women had gone to work in wartime plants all around the country. Edna and Erlene went to Dallas to work in an aircraft plant. Betty Joe was to join them after she graduated. Their mother formed a women's war relief society which did assorted jobs as assigned by a local war assistance board. The men including the reverend and Edward Dumas were busy farming, since everything was in short supply and farms needed to increase production.

Hanghat was in a state of equilibrium for three months, and that was a long period of time for nothing unusual to happen in Hanghat. Only one person and two cows had been struck by lightning, and Guy Malheur and his two authentic offspring, Marie and Au Revoir, had only come or been carried to Dr. Bertram the usual number of times for suturing or bone setting or observation while comatose.

The first indication that things were going to abruptly change was the meeting at city hall by representatives of the federal government and the trustees of the Fissile estate. The trustees were informed that twenty acres of the estate were to be purchased by the federal government for purposes they were not at liberty to discuss. Eminent domain, hush, hush, the check was handed to Baptiste Collage. Baptiste put the check in his safety deposit box to keep the Nazis from finding it.

Jeffie turned red, then went white, and then went blue upon hearing that the government had bought the land where she had been planning to build a party house closer to town for all those invitees with no way to get out to the country when the road was muddy or could become muddy in the future. During her blue phase, she keeled over and died. As she hit the floor, her bouffant wig scurried across the sun porch and knocked over a tray table. Cadet's Undertaking managed to get the wig on her in her coffin, but to do it they had to remove the customary pillow. Baptiste was upset by the idea of his wife spending eternity without the comfort of a pillow, so he asked what could be done to solve the problem. Jeffie was buried in a coffin that was modified to accommodate the wig and the pillow.

Everybody was busy with the war effort and it seemed like no time at all before a large, factory-like building was under construction just beyond the northwest corner of town. A barbed wire fence topped with concertina wire was erected around the building. Onlookers were not allowed past army guard posts, and an army officer warned the town not to gossip about the project, reminding them that the enemy could be listening. Soon the word in Heespud and Tick counties was that secrets were to be tested in a secret building in Hanghat.

Hanghat was growing, the long-waiting businessmen told themselves. Almost as soon as the secret building started going up, a Wiggling Piglet grocery store began construction next door to the shell of the Josephine Theatre.

The real shock came that next week when blasting was heard in the distance, and almost at the same time, sixty truck loads of prefab house parts arrived and parked east of the secret building.

People went to see what the blasting was about and discovered that a railroad track had been laid from Phleville, and that construction had begun on a trestle and a railway up to the uplift. At the cutoff a very large, official-looking sign had been installed by someone. The sign read, "Hanghat, Texas–Dangerous Bridge–Dead End Road." The usual red arrow was at the bottom.

Christmas of 1943 found Hanghat with a looming, great, secret building, a railroad track leading up to the side of the secret building, a fully stocked Wiggling Piglet grocery store, and, next door to the secret building, a grid of paved streets lined with identical, prefabbed, two bedroom homes. A paved street led from the housing development to the road between town and the cutoff. Street signs at the new intersections read, "Cutoff Blvd." and "Project Way."

Hanghatters noticed that Hanghat had no street signs and that the town was yet to pave anything since Main was bricked and 4th through 9th paved for one block each side of Main. An embarrassed chamber of commerce then found money to extend Main's bricks from 2d to 12th and pave the side streets for another two blocks. They stood back and saw that the streets running parallel to Main then needed paving. So, digging deeper and expecting increased business to pay for it, they had those streets paved also. They saved some costs by omitting street signs because everybody knew the streets, anyway, and newcomers could easily learn the few that there were.

Then everyone began to wait for the workers to arrive and move into the new homes and begin their jobs in the secret building. In April a train engine was heard as it pulled the grade up from the trestle and onto the uplift. Hanghatters got as close as the army guards would allow, and they waited until a huge, smoke belching, coal-fired locomotive came into view pulling eight flatcars with their cargo under tarpaulins. Setting atop the tarpaulins on the first and last flatcars was a sandbagged machine gun position with a soldier manning each machine gun along with three other soldiers with rifles. The locomotive squeaked and hissed to a stop when the flatcars were closest to the secret building.

For three days nothing else happened except the soldiers who were off duty would come into town and get haircuts, shop, and drink beer in the Tasting Room. Then on a Friday noon a long line of moving vans arrived accompanied by people in autos. As soon as they came to a stop, furniture was quickly carried into the tract homes. It was an efficient endeavor and by late afternoon emptied vans had gone, leaving the tract's new inhabitants doing yard work and housework and visiting with next door neighbors like they had lived there for days, if not months.

Early the following morning, Hanghat expectantly awaited for an influx of people. The stores had been stocked with goods the newcomers were expected to need, and at eight o'clock the new neighbors began to arrive en mass.

It was the scene that members of the chamber of commerce had imagined a thousand times—autos parked all up and down Main and on the side streets, shoppers filling the business district, and the sidewalks bustling with package toters. Mr. Agneau Jr. ordered his bank teller to climb to the roof of Fissile's Wine Co. to take some photographs of the activities below. Hanghat's population had jumped from 800 to 1055 in one day. The Tasting Room was packed with merrymakers and didn't close until 3:00 a.m.

A week later the town awoke to a sunny day, after a night of rain and thunder and lightning more powerful than usual, to find the soldiers and the flatcars absent. The massive locomotive set at the end of the tracks and the guard posts were deserted.

At the end of that shocking day, a last carload of new inhabitants pulled up to the corner of Cutoff Blvd. and Project Way, turned to the left, and headed away from town; taking their bedding, cookware, and personal items with them, but leaving the furniture.

Hanghat's Brigadoon-like existence continued, but it seemed it wasn't to ever disappear, but, at most, to wake up now and then to supernova with life and merriment between times of isolation from the rest of the world.

The chamber of commerce called the government and the army, but nobody ever found out what had happened, or what the flatcars had carried in and out again, or if the homes were going to be occupied again—and what about the gigantic locomotive setting at the edge of town?

Suddenly, the war was over. Hanghat awaited the return of those who had gone off to do defense work, but only a few returned to live again on the uplift. The secret building and the tract of homes were not the beginnings of a growth spurt, but a precursor of disaster for any plans for a Greater Hanghat.

In the end the town and the uplift lost 25 percent of its prewar population to the jobs and bright lights and fast pace of the big cities. Unbeknownst to Hanghat, the town had already reached its peak population just before WWII began, and would continue to barely manage to hold its population at 600.

CHAPTER 18

Reverend Robert DeBiere died of natural causes in 1945 just after the end of the war with Japan. The three DeBiere children all returned for their father's funeral. Jeanette said that she only had loved two men in her life, Bob Beer and Robert DeBiere, but she loved Robert the more. Not even her children knew Robert was once Bob Beer.

The members of the Hanghat Catheran Church immediately suggested a search for a new minister. Jeanette had worried about the question of what to do now that the Catheran Church's origins and legitimacy were sure to be questioned and exposed by a knowledgeable minister of any faith.

Baptiste Collage was composing a letter requesting the services of a Catheran Minister. It had been decided to send the letter to a Dallas newspaper for publication. Jeanette was preparing to publicly admit that Robert's life work in the Catheran church, and the denomination itself, had been the result of his running from the law. She wanted to confess before the letter was sent, so that the church and the town would not suffer public embarrassment when the outside world asked the inevitable question.

The morning of the day of her confession was when Alfred Beer arrived. Robert's twenty-five year old nephew had departed Los Angeles after receiving Jeanette's letter informing him of the death of his only uncle.

At her house Jeanette told Alfred the whole story, and then, regressing to old behavior brought on by stress, looked at him straight in the chest, waiting for his reply and expecting admonition.

Alfred said nothing. He stood and paced the floor while his right hand covered his thin moustache. If Jeanette had not been looking at the floor while in the arms of guilt, she would have seen Alfred's facial expression as it transited from perplexed to brilliant idea.

Anticipating a rebuke at best, her body jerked slightly as Mr. Beer spoke, "I am, at least I was, a practicing minister in the California-based Church of the Triple Cross. I would be humbled and honored to succeed my uncle in his ministry and continue the traditions and rituals of the church he founded."

Jeanette then escorted Alfred on a tour of the church building, including the basement and its contents.

His first sermon was delivered on the Sunday after Jeanette had instructed him in the procedures of the Catherans and had administered an essay test which he passed with a score of 97. Reverend Beer startled Jeanette when from the pulpit he admitted that his uncle, the Reverend DeBiere, was the Father Founder of the Catheran Church, and that the people of Hanghat had not only witnessed the will of God, but, indeed, had been companions in faith to brother DeBiere who now sat in heaven next to Saint Thomas where he continued to watch over his flock. Then he added that Brother Robert had come to him in a dream and told him that a figure needed to be found to fill the too long unoccupied niche. He had already seen the top half of a carved figure in the dim late afternoon light in the basement, and he planned to install it into the niche.

There was not a dry eye or a humble person in the congregation. They sinfully swelled with pride to be the first Catherans the world of Christendom had ever seen.

The next morning Reverend Beer and Jeanette went to the church basement and, moving junk of all kinds, completely uncovered the statue.

"Oh my god, it's the Mary Magdalene. I had forgotten it."

To Jeanette's relief she saw that the legs were not spread-eagle, as she had come to imagine, but were positioned with the feet together as if the figure had its legs wrapped around something, or, Jeanette hoped not, around somebody.

Alfred shifted the statue off the neatly stacked lumber it had set on through the years, but, when he moved the statue, it knocked down a row of lumber, revealing an edge of a crate. He removed the layer of boards setting on the crate's hinged top, then raised it. Rusted hinges peeped and chirped like cheerful canaries. Inside were a cello and its bow, and a baby Jesus that was obviously the work by the sculptor of the church's other statuary.

Jeanette looked over at the Magdalene, and for the first time noticed that its hands were positioned as if playing a cello, and the left hand wasn't missing a goblet of wine, but was meant to be around the cello's neck. She sighed, "It's just a statue of a cellist. Thank God."

"It's amazing," said Alfred, "It's not Mary Magdalene at all, unless she played the cello. I don't think it had been invented in Roman times."

Jeanette inspected the face on the statue, and then she remembered Eclaire's telling of the tale of the Coupable family—Don Roscoe Culpable's mother had played a cello. Eclaire had told her daughters the entire saga of Laverne Rognan Coupable who had, according to a report in a letter from the old parish, died while furiously swatting during an all night attack by a gigantic swarm of hungry mosquitoes.

She suddenly exclaimed, "You're correct. This isn't Mary Magdalene. It's the sculpture's mother, a woman who was called from Hanghat by God to alleviate the suffering of the poor living under holey mosquito nets in the Louisiana bayous."

Albert Beer, looking puzzled at Jeanette, asked her, "What is a holy mosquito net . . . a blessed net?"

"No," replied Jeanette, "she gave away unholey mosquito nets; new mosquito nets that had no holes in them. When I said holey, I meant with holes."

"Oh, I see. Excuse me, I've had only religion on my mind since I arrived . . . and I heard holey as holy. You say she helped the poor and died in the service of God?"

"Yes."

"Well, this is a great day, then. Think about it. The Catheran Church has its first saint. Saint Laverne of the Unholey Nets . . . No. How about of the Holy Nets? No, too confusing. I've got it—Saint Laverne of the Bayous."

Reverend Beer got Marshal LeConte, Joy LeConte's first born, to help carry Saint Laverne's likeness and place it in the chair that had waited empty for all those years. Reverend Beer then placed the baby Jesus in the arms of the Mary in the vestibule.

The next Sunday Saint Laverne of the Bayou set with cello. The reverend told the story of her life and good works, then, by a show of hands, Laverne was unanimously elected to be the first official saint in the Catheran Church.

Two days before Christmas of 1945, Jeanette was thinking about her children and reminiscing. Alone in her house Jeanette downed a second glass of white Bordeaux. She rationalized aloud and listened to herself, "It is sure that more twits had been born as a result of my withholding the truth, hiding it, but who comes into this world, after all, should only be determined by God—not Jeanette. No, not me. Anyway, it is out of my hands."

She continued talking to herself while she decided to play some Christmas songs on the phonograph. "Why won't it turn on?" she asked herself.

The sober self she spoke to saw that the plug had come loose, and she bent down to replace it in its outlet. Then, just as she touched the plug to the outlet, lightning a quarter mile away traveled down the power lines and out the outlet and through Jeanette's long term memory storage, with a ripple of current also rearranging connections in her short term circuits; leaving her absent of any doubts about her decision concerning Sire. She staggered, then recovered and put the Andrew's Sisters on the phonograph, set the needle arm in place, and flipped the 'on' switch. "Why won't it start? Oh, I see. It's unplugged."

As it was, nobody in town could then remember to open the time capsule. The pedestal containing it had not been seen through trees and a dense tangle of underbrush since 1905. In 1946 a 'For Sale' sign was placed on the Main Street side of the city block known locally as, "The Thicket."

Among those who returned to the uplift after the war's end were the three Dumas girls, Edna Mae, Erlene Louise, and Betty Joe. Erlene had returned as Mrs. Crawford MacGregor. She had married a product engineer whom she had met at work. Edna Mae, saving herself for marriage, had dated and fought off several ardent suitors, one of whom had her down to her slip and bra when his mother phoned and ruined the mood. Edna Mae had been unlucky in love while working in Dallas.

Once when fourteen years old, Edna, upon becoming alarmed by the physical changes and naughty thoughts brought about by puberty, practiced piety and made promises to St. Thomas during a month long spree of three confessions per day. She told him that she would become a nun in the Catheran church, but Reverend DeBiere told her that the Catherans had no orders of nuns, and suggested that Edna Mae wait until completing school before making any decisions.

Betty Joe, being the youngest, only eighteen in 1944, was carefully chaperoned by her two older sisters, giving her no chances for any kind of luck with love.

Of the Malheur children who had departed, Luc and Guy were to remain in the navy, Jean and John and Belle and Helene would remain in the big city, and Gigi and Leo would become permanent Hanghatters. Marie and little Au Revoir were usually recovering from some physical catastrophe, as was their father, and they only thought about the outside world during idle interludes of convalescence. Gigi replaced her mother, Maude, at the switchboard, because years of pushing in and pulling out phone jacks had given Maude arthritis and a carpel tunnel that rivaled the entrance to the Comstock Load. Mr. Malheur, working from a wheelchair, continued his job at Cadet's Barber Shop & Undertaking.

Edna Mae Dumas had become a woman of opinion and a woman who got things done. Upon her return to town she immediately went to work writing letters and making phone calls to the federal and state governments in attempts to discover what was to be done with the secret building, the locomotive, and the tract homes that still set unoccupied and still contained the furniture the vans had delivered.

All replies to her questions denied the existence of any government facility or locomotive in the areas of Heespud and Tick counties, and, furthermore, the replies would say that Hanghat, Texas was not even on their maps.

At the county courthouse she could not find any record of any sale of Fissile Trust property to the federal government. Hanghat and the uplift farms had been on the county tax rolls since the election of 1932 when the people had registered to vote, causing the county to become aware of them again. Edna found the twenty acres that the government had supposedly bought to have outstanding taxes owed by the owner, one Fissile Trust, so she paid the $75 right on the spot and got a notarized receipt.

Edna then decided to go inside the fence surrounding the secret building and investigate the interior. She had the grandson of the original Chevel of Chevel's Blacksmith cut a gate lock, then Edna and a reluctant Erlene marched into the building, which they found open and entirely empty—no machines, no crates, no secrets, no anything but a smooth concrete floor and white painted walls of sheet metal. It was built like an aircraft hanger—there were no interior posts—just a completely clear expanse of floor measuring 150 by 200 feet under a 40-foot high ceiling.

With nothing to see in the secret building, they went out to inspect the locomotive. It set at the end of a long paved street which had the tracks running down the center. They found wasp nests in the cab, and coal in the tender.

They then walked over to the close-by, tract homes and looked into some windows. The yards were overgrown and paper and garbage were everywhere, but the furnished houses were clean inside and seemed to be waiting for their occupants to get home from work.

Edna looked at her sister and said, "As far as I can determine this land still is Fissile property, and as the trustee I'm going to clean it up, starting with having that ugly fence taken down. Either that or make this into the largest chicken coop in Texas."

The townsfolk came and explored the building and its surroundings after the fence was removed, then at a city council meeting the next week it was decided that the twenty acres the building and tract homes occupied would be annexed by the city. Hanghat would grow in size, if not population.

Rumor was that the government would show up and claim the land, but that never happened. The street with the locomotive was named Train Street and it was extended to connect with the west end of 2nd Street. Calls to every railroad in Texas couldn't find the owner of the locomotive or someone to stoke the boilers and haul it away—it was an older and unwanted model. The tract homes were arrayed with a goodly number of lightning rods and boarded-up.

Baptiste Collage sold Collage Department Store and retired in 1946. He had lived alone in Fissile House since Jeffie's death from the shock of being thwarted by the government. Sunshine, always an attentive daughter, visited him often and insisted that her three daughters do the same. Baptiste, nevertheless, died of melancholy in 1946, and the following month, Erlene and her husband moved into Fissile House against their wishes. Erlene considered the house too big to be comfortable in, and her husband didn't want to leave their house in town where he had set up his research laboratory.

According to Overte's will, as long as a family member lived in the mansion, the grand house would remain a private residence. All the artworks in Fissile House, as part of the trust agreement, were to remain a part of the estate, and Fissile House was to be opened to public view for one weekend every six months.

Erlene quickly came to enjoy the extra space, and Crawford was to enjoy his bigger laboratory in what had been a first floor sitting room just off the kitchen.

Crawford continued work on developing his latest invention; one spurred on by his constant encounters with the uplift's lightning. He had foreseen his being struck by lightning and being instantly vaporized to float off the side of the uplift as a wisp of cloud that smelled like burning hair.

He was on the back porch monitoring his fifth improved version of his Lightning Bypass Umbrella as a thunderstorm approached. In the yard his test umbrella was open and mounted in rings on a post representing a person carrying it. The tip of the umbrella was a lightning rod, and the shaft and handle were made of copper.

Trailing from the bottom of the handle to the ground was a copper chain covered with braided leather to make it stylish. If everything went as planned, any lightning bolt striking the top of the umbrella would be conducted safely down the shaft, then down the trailing stylish tail to be dissipated in the ground. A chicken 'guinea pig' tethered to a stake under the umbrella pecked at the ground and clucked calmly, seemingly unconcerned that it had seen four other chickens in the same situation fried by lightning.

Just before the storm arrived, the chicken, which had been biding her time waiting for the right moment, violently flapped her wings and flew away with the stake dangling behind.

A true scientist wonders for a moment about how a plump red hen could fly like a wild turkey, then he ignores personal safety when some last second, chicken re-staking is needed to save a trial run, especially a trial run of a device that he is sure will work on this fifth test, so there actually is no danger qua danger, as it were, but the test must have all its parts in place, anyway.

Mr. Cadet Jr. insisted that Erlene take advantage of the "Death By Lightning" special he had been offering since Mr. Cadet Sr. had been struck in 1932 while doing business in Hanghat's graveyard.

Erlene mourned for a year during which time she sent for Edna so often that by the end of that year Edna had moved into Fissile House with her.

Betty Joe remained in Hanghat in a house at

the east end of 12th Street, a block from the fairgrounds. She was the daughter who most favored Sunshine in her appearance. Whereas Edna had her mother's crusading spirit without a desire for travel, Betty Joe daydreamed of the excitement of distant places but wanted to be near her family, and that caused ambivalence, leaving her often feeling unfulfilled with her life in Hanghat. All that she needed to make a change was a catalyst to come her way, something that would carry her away to a new life; a force so compelling that in its persuasion there would be no leftover remorse for being swept away from Hanghat. For Betty Joe as for most young women that force was almost always a young man—or a baby elephant.

The Uplift Fair was held at the fairgrounds every October. The usual exhibits of prize livestock and prize quilts and prize pies, cakes, and jams were expected again in 1948, but that year a small carnival with a big attraction came to the fairgrounds and raised a small big top and setup a small Ferris wheel and a pony ride. By any measure it was a broken-down outfit, but it had elephants.

Everybody able to go made it to the fair. Sunshine and Edward met their daughters at Betty Joe's house. Sunshine had made a blackberry pie for the competition, so the family departed and walked directly to the 'Cakes and Pies' tent where Sunshine registered her pie and placed it on the pie table. Betty Joe had gone to pet the elephants.

The carnival people after many years of

experience in small towns around Texas and Oklahoma and Arkansas were pretty sure they had seen about everything, but Hanghat was a storehouse of the unexpected.

Inside the just big enough big top, the Dumas family gathered to watch the show. A parade of the animals began and went off without a hitch as a mother elephant and her two year old baby led a procession of pony-ride ponies followed by what looked like a diminutive and mangy lion in a cage pulled by two men. Behind the cage came a trained dog act followed by the carnival employees wearing red coats over work clothes and playing various brass instruments and beating the side of a bass drum that didn't have the hole in it.

The parade circled the ring and went out the tent flap they had entered, then the best-dressed person of the group, wearing white pants, red jacket, and shine-less patent leather boots, announced, "And now di-re-e-e-ct from Belgium, Hans Brechte and his fabulous canines."

Well, a fabulous bitch or two was in heat and had attracted a pack of Spots. Brechte's canines entered the ring followed by the Spots, and dogs began to hump dogs and people's legs and the tent poles. Dog fights broke out and dogs and carnival workers were running in every direction.

The laughing crowd watched the hullabaloo. Edward Dumas escorted his family out the way they had entered. They were out of the tent in time to see the elephants panic and run across the street and into Betty Joe's backyard.

Their handler, already drunk, had been knocked down and didn't seem able to get back onto his feet. The panicked elephants were out of control, with the mother mock charging toward anybody who approached in their direction.

People began to shout, "Mad elephant," and the situation was becoming dangerous when the baby began to walk toward Betty Joe who was standing closest to it. Betty Joe stood there not knowing exactly what she should do. The baby came and nuzzled her and lifted his trunk and took her hand, leading her back to its mother, who calmed down and began to eat a branch she tore from an elm.

The fair lasted its usual three days. On the fourth day, with the elephant's keeper still woozy from a head injury, Betty Joe ran away with the circus. Her note to her family read, "I couldn't stand to see that baby elephant and his mother mistreated by the people who tried to get them into their trailer. They followed me right in. I'll be back as soon as their keeper recovers from his injury. Love, Betty Joe."

Her parents and sisters received regular letters from such places as San Angelo and Mexia, Texas, then she wrote that the elephant act had been added to a big time circus, and the letters soon came with big city postmarks from Atlanta to Denver.

Nineteen forty-nine came and went as a year of gathering energy. Betty Joe's letters came regularly, but the circus wintered in Florida and she couldn't make it home that year. Jeanette, who didn't remember anything about her accident with the phonograph plug, was considered to have suddenly become senile. She remembered events occurring since that night with the Andrews Sisters, but her long term memories were vague and not always accessible.

Twenty-one year-old Bernadette LeConte became the June bride of Reverend Alfred Beer in 1949. Nobody knew that Bernadette was the biological daughter of Edward Dumas; not even Edward.

Edward had continued meeting Joy LeConte through the years in an easily climbed magnolia tree growing beside the rectory. Joy would climb up from the ground, stepping on the horizontal branches growing like stairs, to find Edward. Then, with the lovers standing on a same branch, she would lean back against a higher branch, and they would mate in the tree like monkeys who had learned the missionary position.

Nobody seemed to notice how similar Bernadette's personality was to those of her unsuspected half-sisters. Edna, Erlene and Betty Joe did seem more like Genevieve and her side of the family, but only because the three, having loved and admired their mother, had succeeded in emulating her mannerisms and laughter, even successfully learning to stifle a snicker which could prove so embarrassing in the presence of young men. All four women, however, had the same color and shape of eyes and identical eyelashes, and the same way of reacting when upset, and this latter attribute was a paternal trait.

But, of course, everybody in Hanghat was accustomed to the fact that many of them looked and acted alike, and many still attributed the similarities to be the results of drinking the local water.

CHAPTER 19

A son, Robert Olin Beer, was born to Bernadette and Alfred on February 1, 1951.

The new decade was one of promise, Hanghat told itself. The chamber of commerce had Monday night brainstorming sessions that would keep the Tasting Room open till after midnight. Suggestions included the building of an airport and the old standby idea of luring a factory. Again letters were sent out and unanswered.

The town was still losing momentum, however. That spring saw the Wiggling Piglet take its groceries and shelves and leave town. That was an economic downturn, but a tragedy occurred while the big Wiggling Piglet sign with the wiggling neon tail was being taken down. Marie Malheur came limping down the sidewalk to be directly under the piglet when it came loose from ropes and fell smack on her head.

The accident left only two true Malheurs in town—Guy, her father, and her younger brother, Au Revoir. Guy would succumb to what had become known as the Malheur curse a month later when he, in his wheelchair, would fall out of a tree. Even though he had landed right-side-up, the chair accelerated downhill and hurled Guy off the cliff overlooking the 9th Street swimming hole on Parish Creek. He should have hit the water, but kids at the swimming hole who saw the flying wheelchair said that it seemed to gain altitude as it crossed the creek and then dropped, once it was above the opposite bank.

Guy's demise left twenty-two year old Au Revoir as the only recipient of the energetic and now deadly Malheur curse. With Dr. Bertram's skill as a remover of quarter-pound splinters and resuscitator of the unconscious, Au Revoir was still alive when the Wiggling Piglet company paid the family a sum of money for Marie's death.

Au Revoir then had a three room, redoubt-style bunker built on the southeast edge of town. The home had balsa and corkwood furniture, fifteen pole-mounted lightning rods, and no kitchen or stove or electricity. He made arrangements with the general store for deliveries of groceries and necessities, then declared that he intended to stay in his accident-resistant home and never come out.

Well-wishers including Dr. Bertram and Edna said au revoir Au Revoir, then Au Revoir shut and barred his door. Dr. Bertram, who still had to remove the cast on Au Revoir's right leg, would be the last person to see him for several years, but people knew he was alive because deliveries from the general store would be gone shortly after being placed by the bunker's steel door.

Edna, meanwhile, had come up with an idea to put Hanghat on the map—literally. She presented her plan at the Monday night brainstorming session. Her plan was to turn the secret building into the largest roller rink in Texas. When she completed her presentation by unveiling a sketch showing a thousand rollerskaters on the floor of a 30,000 square foot rink, with adjoining snack bars and dressing rooms, the chamber of commerce stood and cheered, then tasted wine till the a.m.

The secret building became the Hanghat Roller Rink in 1952, and the huge sign erected at the cutoff by the government was repainted to read, "Hanghat: Home Of The Biggest Roller Rink In Texas." The mandatory arrow was at the bottom, but was stylized as a roller skate, and beneath the roller skate arrow was the fear-lessening claim, "The Bridge Is Not Dangerous."

Opening day and 300 new faces arrived in Hanghat along with one familiar face—Betty Joe had come home to visit, and happened to come in time for the big event.

To commemorate the grand opening, as well as the belief of it being a new day dawning in Hanghat's struggle for growth, the great locomotive was to move backward until it was away from the entrance to the rink. A banner tied to its side read, "Hanghat—A City On The Move."

A search for a driver had turned up Conklin, an eighty year-old man who said he was a retired locomotive engineer from the T & P Railroad. Early morning on the big day, Conklin was boosted up the ladder and helped into the cab. His weak and gravely voice ordered a water hose to begin filling the engine's tank, and he gave his fireman, Moody Marlin, the current chamber of commerce president, instructions on how to start the fire box with kindling, then told him to start shoveling coal.

Moody, who was suspicious about the old man's abilities, decided that the old engineer, indeed, knew what he was doing. What Moody Marlin didn't know was that Conklin only remembered a career as an engineer, when, actually, he had never made it past being a stoker because he was not gifted at valve turning or the pulling of the correct lever.

The Hanghat Roller Rink, ribbon-cutting ceremony was to be at 11:00 a.m., and, as soon as the ribbon was cut, the engine, decorated with American flags and crepe paper, was to sound its whistle, ring its bell, and move backward to a position where it was to set permanently as an attraction.

At 10:00 a.m. Edna drove up in her new 1952 Dodge sedan with Erlene and Betty Joe and Jeanette. At 10:58 Edna Mae was ready to cut the ribbon. A newspaper reporter and photographer from Heespud City were ready to record the story. The mighty engine was belching dark gray smoke. The old pseudo-engineer's hand was poised on a lever. The Hanghat High Hedgehog marching band watched the drum major for the signal to begin Sousa's "Stars And Stripes Forever."

The mayor completed a speech, Edna cut the red curly ribbon, the band began playing, and the locomotive spun its driving wheels and began to move in the wrong direction and toward the end of the tracks two hundred feet ahead. The tracks stopped where Train Street turned left to join 2nd. Across the street was Parish Creek, and the train was picking up speed. Moody's hand had pulled the chord to toot the whistle, and it was frozen in that position, sounding a constant blast as Moody's eyes grew larger and larger.

The flags decorating the locomotive were fluttering when the train ran out of track and dug its way across the roadway. It was downhill for the seventy-five feet from the road to the bank of the creek. The locomotive with its drive wheels still driving went down the slope and, with grating, earth shaking sounds heard above the loud continuous whistle, it splashed into the creek and smashed into the opposite bank, bulldozing into it for about ten feet. A large hole was gashed in the boiler causing a geyser of steam which whoofed the "Hanghat—A City On The Move" banner high into the air.

Moody finally came out of shock, his eyes had returned to normal size, and he assisted Conklin out of the cab and waded to shore carrying the old man who was complaining that some sneak had switched levers on him.

The locomotive and tender, along with the considerable debris of whole trees and a massive volume of dirt and rock, formed a dam, and the creek began to back up. By sundown two days later, a lake had filled and was spilling over through the locomotive's cab window. A large catfish had moved from his pool upstream to the deeper water where he took up residence down deep in the recesses of the boiler.

The rink's opening day was also the day of the biggest theft in Hanghat's history, for, while downtown shops were closed for just two hours for the ribbon cutting ceremony, somebody had entered the general store and absconded with the last fifty, blue, U.S. Cavalry (in yellow stitched letters) war surplus, horse blankets of the sixty originally bought by Sans Foudre. The thief left payment for the pilfered blankets, but it was at least breaking and entering, so Hanghat at the next town meeting voted for Marshal LeConte as town sheriff. Sheriff Marshal LeConte went straight to work on the blanket crime. His thorough investigation and interrogations legally proved that the blankets were missing from the shelf in the general store where he had been seeing them since he could remember.

Two days later in Indianapolis, Indiana, loose meat sandwich shop owners, Al and Gertrude Sampson, sat at their breakfast table reading the newspaper when they ran across an article about the grand opening of the largest roller rink in Texas. The piece included a photo of a train splashing into water. In the large photo was a small insert photo of the skating rink. The Samson's loose meat sandwich business was not growing, and another competitor was opening close to their once prime, loose meat location, so the loose meat couple had already been thinking about a new business in another part of the country. Al and Gertrude had previously been reading the business and franchise opportunity magazines, and they had sent off and received information about a new company called, Daisy Queen.

They wrote the Queen's headquarters and

were told they had no outlet in Hanghat. The Queen's headquarters indicated that they would be glad to have someone with food business experience open a Queen in the town with the biggest roller rink in Texas. The research department at Queen corporate headquarters searched maps for Hanghat, Texas for two days to even find out where it was.

Al and Gertrude drove from an icy December Indianapolis to the mild climate of Hanghat. They visited the roller rink and then went to the bank to find out if the bank thought a Queen would be a success, and to discuss a loan.

Rumor was that Phleville and Haygap already had Queens scheduled, so the bank pounced on the opportunity of making a business loan when the Samsons came calling.

The site the Samsons wanted to build on was overgrown with poison oak. Al said that Gertrude was allergic to it and the lot was too expensive. Then, Al asked, "What about a Main Street lot a few blocks south of downtown? Should be cheaper, shouldn't it?"

In 1953 the first Queen in Hanghat was open for business, and, just as in other one Queen, Texas towns, it quickly became the place to be and to be seen.

The Samsons had no difficulty making the transition from a loose meat to a tight meat, and the Hanghat Queen was successful from the first day. The south location was closer to the school, so more kids came in, and farmers and families had to pass the Queen coming and going when they shopped downtown.

The Hanghat Roller Rink never got rolling. There was little business after the first month. The decreasing radius, reverse cambered curve and the fifteen mile distance from Phleville deterred most who thought about skating a second time in Texas's largest rink, and Hanghatters were not attracted to indoor, unseated activities. The attempt at placing skates on the legs of mazettes was an abject failure.

Betty Joe had visited for three days on that first trip back to Hanghat from the circus, then, one year later she returned again, and with a baby girl. She said nothing about the father, and nobody asked her about him, but, since the baby was three months old, the rumor was that she had done more than just attend a grand opening when last in Hanghat.

Betty Joe arrived just in time to assist her great-aunt, Jeanette. The 82 year old was having a difficult time living alone, even though she insisted upon doing just that. Betty Joe and her baby moved in with her, and the three lived together with no problems. Jeanette was dowager's humpless thanks to a diet sufficient in greens which she had grown for years in a garden behind her house, and she was able to move around semi-gracefully, even if she would often forget why she had left one room and gone to another. Betty Joe was also a great help in occasionally dislodging a neighborhood Spot which had recently been humping on Jeanette while she gardened.

The 1950's ended with Hanghatters wanting to know who were the Phantom Lovers who had first begun to purposely leave evidence of their daring liaisons in the winter of 1956.

The first love scene was found in the middle of Texas' biggest roller rink on a Saturday morning in December. Sheriff Marshal discovered the scene when he came to open the rink for a school skate party.

There in the flat-dab middle of the rink was one of the missing horse blankets all spread out next to two empty wine glasses and an empty quart Mason jar that smelled like it had contained something alcoholic.

Sheriff Marshal squatted and ran his hand through a small pile of dried rose petals on the blanket. His hand felt something and he lifted it into view and yelled, "Sacre bleu, a damned rubber." It was the first sacre bleu exclaimed in Hanghat for at least ten years. He quickly wiped his fingers on the blanket as he added, "A used rubber . . . what is goin' on here?"

He went outside and returned with a stick and fished the rubber onto it. He carried it outside, dug a hole with the heel of his boot and buried the rubber. He then gathered the remaining evidence in the blanket and carried it to his 1955 Chevrolet Belaire. He placed it in the trunk and drove down Train Street past Train Lake and its huge catfish hovering in its depths within the boiler of the dam.

At his office, a room partitioned off from the meeting room in city hall, he inspected the evidence once more, then placed it on a shelf.

By the end of Catheran services that Sunday, the word was out that the sheriff was looking for two people who had entered the roller rink Friday night and left a mess that included one of the fifty missing horse blankets.

Two weeks later on a Saturday morning the Hanghat Ladies' Club was in the city hall when Sheriff Marshal came in and found his office unlocked.

Shortly after he entered his door he exclaimed, "They've done it again. Right in my office on top my desk."

The ladies watched as the sheriff went outside carrying something wrapped in newspaper.

He came back in and addressed the ladies, "The ones that broke into the roller rink have done the same thing in my office . . . in my office," he added emphatically. He started for his office while saying, "I want your ladies to look at this stuff and see if you know where it came from."

He returned to the table where the ladies sat, and placed a horse blanket bundle on the table, and opened it. The women stared at the contents—two wine glasses, a mess of dried rose petals, and an almost empty quart canning jar with its lid in place.

Genevieve, Edna, Erlene and the other women shook their heads, indicating they had no idea about the origin of the items.

Edna said, "Isn't that like one of the missing horse blankets?"

Sheriff Marshal replied, "I do suspect it is

just that . . . just that. And right in my personal office, too, right on top my desk . . . right on top my dadburn desk."

The women had no idea why the sheriff was so upset. He looked at them as if he was waiting to be consoled. With puzzled expressions they looked at him, then at the objects, back and forth several times.

The sheriff had FL as great-grandfather on both branches of his family tree, and it was that unknown begetter whose legacy had predisposed Sheriff Marshal to be at first stimulated, then indifferent about the first blanket party. He had let the roller rink episode slip from his mind as an active case to be pursued, but, then, they did it on his desk.

Still fuming, he blurted, "Somebody did it on top my desk last night after I left my office. They're not doin' it outside like decent people would. . . . Here," he unscrewed the lid of the quart jar, "smell this. I think it's something homemade . . . maybe you know something about where it came from."

The jar passed around and under noses attached to heads which nodded, no, then Edna handed it to Jeanette.

The distinctive aroma unshocked vivid memories. "Honeyberry brew," Jeanette said, then deeply inhaled a second time. "Honeyberry brew and noble rot. I remember this. The warren. I remember it all. Somebody has kept this a long long time. It was shameful, what we did. Those poor artists. Poor Guy Vin Gough. August 22,

1921 was the day we picked it clean."

Jeanette held the jar up to the light. There was about a quarter inch of brew in the bottom, which she suddenly and quickly swigged. She wiped her mouth with her shawl and commented, "And it was fortified, too." She smacked her lips and said, "I think, with brandy."

The sheriff, disgusted, said, "Oh, Mrs. DeBiere that was evidence . . . that was evidence."

CHAPTER 20

The art sanctuary had been abandoned since a final, landscape painter and his potter wife departed for Houston in 1951. The sanctuary's high rock wall was covered in vines of all sorts including poison oak. A maze of narrow paths inside the walls led through a woods of scrub oak and cedar to connect derelict small dwellings built from odds and ends, all stylized and angular, or rounded, and obviously designed by the imaginations of artists.

In 1960 a representative of a Baptist brotherhood organization came to Hanghat in search of a retreat site for his group known as the Southern Baptist Authoritarians (SBA). Moody Marlin, who was president of Agneau Bank and Realty, took the Baptist man to look at the abandoned, art sanctuary.

The man said that it might be too small for the group's activities, but possibly not. He departed after dinner with Moody in the Biscuit Café—the former Le Bistro renamed by Terry LeConte to sound more like a place to eat, rather than to drink absinthe and watch apache dancing.

A month after the visit from the SBA man, a married couple was in town looking for a location for their organization, and they met with the only realtor in town.

Moody Marlin sitting behind his new genuine mahogany veneer desk got up and shook their hands and asked, "What is it today, folks,

banking or real estate?"
The couple said they were looking for secluded property as a site for the SBA, then, before they could explain what the SBA was, Moody interrupted them.

"Oh yes, the SBA. I'd be a member myself, but I'm not of that persuasion. Well, the perfect site for an organization like yours is still available. The Fissile Trust has the same firm price on it, though. Have you personally been by there, yet? Let's go see how it's looking."

The SBA couple especially liked the high wall and told Moody that it was a done deal.

"Of course, we won't put up any signs or advertise or anything like that, and all business will be conducted in my name just like it will be on the deed," said the SBA representative when he signed the sales agreement a week later at the property site. Moody had finally sold a piece of property.

"The real estate business is really going to take off," he said, as he and his wife Minna ate at the Biscuit that same afternoon. Just as he spoke those words, in walked the man from the SBA who had originally looked at the art sanctuary.

Moody stood up, shook his hand and said, "Congratulations on your purchase."

"What purchase?" replied the man.

"Why, the old art sanctuary. Your SBA representative bought it himself, just today."

"What! That must have been the SBA from the Bralm, Alabama Second Synod of 1899. Did you ask him what synod he was from? I thought I saw one or two of them when our church discussed this location at Sunday service."

Moody looked surprised, and in defense he replied, "We're all Catherans here; don't know about synods. Didn't know to ask."

The man thought he had heard Moody say that the townspeople were all Catholics, and asked, "All of you, everyone in town?"

"Every last one of us. The church was created right here in Hanghat by Brother Robert."

The man did not know what to say to that, but thought it explained why everyone in town looked him straight in the chest while he spoke—they were obviously wondering if he was wearing a crucifix.

"I should have known they would connive and find out we had found a perfect spot for a retreat," declared the now red-faced man of a different synod. "Well, I'll show them. Do you have any other property like that for sale up here?"

The angry man spent the night at Anne's Rooms. The next day he signed a contract to buy five acres at the east end of 11th Street.

As he walked out of Moody's office he turned and said, "There, that'll show them, we've got one more acre. Yes, sir, it'll be a cold day below God's green earth when those second synod heretics put something over on the Bralm's First Synod of 1899 and think they can get away with it. How high is their wall?"

"I think it's twelve feet," replied Moody.

"Well then, we're going thirteen . . . maybe fourteen," said the synodically angry man who then shut the door hard. A second later he opened the door again, and added, “Why don’t you people put up some street signs so our congregation can know where to turn to get there?”

“Never been any need,” Moody replied. “Everybody knows where the streets are; just tell your people to turn left at the Daisy Queen and go straight to the property.”

Another wall went up around the five acres belonging to the Bralm’s first synoders, and by the following summer both walled retreats were full of retreaters.

Hanghatters heard or saw nothing but laughter or volleyballs coming over the walls of the SBA at the end of 3rd Street. Its women members came into town wearing light, summery dresses revealing their backs and their knees, and sometimes they would shop in their bathing suits. They were all tanned and full of energy and very outgoing. They would buy beer and wine, and toys for their children, and spent lots of money each summer during their three month series of two week retreats.

They were secretive, however, and no Hanghatters ever knew of anybody from town ever being invited in or ever being allowed inside the walls, but almost everybody in Hanghat had decided that if they ever quit the Catherans and became Baptists, then they would definitely join the group of Bralm’s second synoders.

The 11th street SBA was different. Preaching could be heard beyond the fourteen foot walls. The members were not tanned and never bought beer or wine, but were avid buyers of wieners and mustard and hot dog buns. When asked if they had a swimming pool one of the 11th Street Synoders, as Hanghatters had come to call them, replied that it was ungodly to have such a thing at a church retreat.

The Baptists, thinking that Hanghatters were all Catholics, were brief but polite in their encounters, and just as unwilling as the other SBA to allow locals inside their walls.

CHAPTER 21

Hanghat had no swimming pool, but it did have Train Lake, and every day during summer just about every kid in Hanghat would go swimming there. The younger kids were there early in the day, then by late afternoon the teenagers would take over, and the smaller kids, not wanting to be dunked or thrown in repeatedly, would vacate the lake and walk upstream to a small pool where the water was just deep enough to swim but not to dive into.

It was noon on a summer in 1962 when it happened. The catfish living in the boiler had weighed around twenty pounds when it first swam to Train Lake. By the summer of 1962 the fish had grown to weigh 200 pounds, and it had developed an appetite requiring more than the fish and turtles and algae it had fed on.

Luckily, the attempted swallowing came just after the older, bigger kids had started to arrive. Two high school football players were spreading out blankets, while their dates got things out of their car, when they heard splashing and a frantic call for help from a skinny six year old kid in the lake. All anybody could see was a giant white mouth opening and closing between two little black eyes. Inside the mouth was the kid's right leg. Then the fish unswallowed the leg and bumped up against the boy to get the wildly thrashing meal in position to swallow it.

The two footballers jumped in and grabbed the kid's arms. Then, after a bit of tug of war, the giant catfish turned loose and returned to the solitude of its boiler abode.

The almost-swallowed kid was hysterical, and everybody large and small had already gotten out of the lake, wondering what had just happened. One kid said it was the Devil, but whatever it was, they decided it had been as real as the bleeding scrapes on the thigh of the almost-swallowed kid.

Townsmen in a boat searched the lake that day, and searched with flashlights from the shore that night, but no monstrous thing could be found.

Edna and Erlene were at the lake on the second day of the search. Betty Joe and her daughter, nine year old Pauline, had accompanied them while Jeanette napped at home.

The searchers in boats were throwing out lines with large hooks baited with chunks of fish and beef, when Betty Joe commented, “It’s a shame they have to hook it. They could kill it before they know what it is. Why, in the circus if it’s something unusual it would become an attraction.”

Edna Mae, the manager of the biggest and emptiest roller rink in Texas, saw an idea immediately and ran to the edge of the water yelling, “Don’t kill it! Don’t kill it! It could be valuable. I’m going to go get Moody. I’ll be right back. And get those shark hooks out of the lake.”

By late afternoon a crowd stood on the bank while two men in a boat threw a bag full of liver and fish tied to the end of a chord. They were trying to get the creature to gulp down the bag.

They hoped to hold the monster at the surface long enough to see what it was.

All eyes were on the bait bag when a giant mouth emerged and engulfed it. The man holding the chord was pulled into the lake while someone shouted, "It's a catfish! A really big catfish!"

"I think you've got a draw, sister," said Betty Joe. "Come see the biggest roller rink in Texas, and the man-eater in the nearby lake."

"It wouldn't be a lie, either," said Erlene, "That damned thing would have eaten little Exel if those boys hadn't pulled him out of its mouth."

"Working around circus acts taught me some animal training tricks," said Betty Joe. "I'll have him coming up to eat when we want him to."

Down at the cutoff, the sign was repainted with the added words "See the giant man-eater. Watch the monster eat at 9A.M. and Noon. (Extra moonlight feeding during full moons). Roller Rink & Monster Open On Saturdays & Sundays ONLY."

That first Saturday Edna and Erlene were at the rink early, but only eight customers showed up, and they only wanted to see the monster eat.

It was Moody Marlin's idea to place a second sign where Tick County Road 4 met the state highway. Edna Mae made a deal with the farmer at the junction and leased a space for a second sign. The following few months saw a doubling of business, but twice as much of too little was not enough to keep the rink open and feed the monster, who seemed to have become a picky gourmand, only coming up for properly aged liver and steak combos.

The kids missed swimming in the lake until one of the young men who had just returned from four years of college figured out that the catfish would not try to swallow anybody of a certain minimum size. Then the man suggested it would be wise to keep the beast well fed.

Swimmers returned to the lake in the summer of '63. A plank was made into a seesaw with a heavy rock tied on one end. Small swimmers who questionably could have been catfish meals would sit on the seesaw, and if their weight lifted the rock then they could swim with the catfish, without fear of being ingested. When the plank broke, the seesaw test was replaced by a mark on a sign reading, "The Catfish Can't Eat You If You Are This Tall."

The fish was tamed by the end of that swimming season, and it would take scraps from the Biscuit and the Queen right out of people's hands.

Edna Mae thought about adding words to the signs on County Road 4 saying, "Hand Feed The Monster Catfish," but the idea quickly passed. Her entrepreneuring days were over, she decided, until a sure fire idea came along.

CHAPTER 22

The Phantom Lovers began leaving a greeting card on each abandoned, horse blanket. By January 1964 Sheriff Marshal had collected fifteen blankets of evidence from what were increasingly more daring locations. Each card was signed, "The Phantom Lovers," and included messages with comments about how exciting it was to do it naked on the roof of the mayor's house and in the hallway of the high school, etcetera.

Sheriff Marshal eventually persuaded himself that it was his job to put an end to the affair, even if that meant the end of the hottest topic in town. Seeking leads, the sheriff had visited all the local merchants in Heespud and Tick counties, but he couldn't find any orange candles like the ones the Phantom Lovers always left behind.

On his office wall Sheriff Marshal had a map of Hanghat with pins marking the matings. He had read enough detective stories to know that the criminal always returns to the scene of the crime, so he would make the rounds to each most recent Phantom Lover's site every night. He was obsessed with the idea of their arrest and conviction on some charges he couldn't quite decide on, but something like trespassing or possession of stolen property or public lewdness seemed in order. The latter, he decided, may not be a valid charge, since nobody had ever seen them doing it. At least, he told himself, nobody had ever admitted to seeing the Lovers engaged in their naughty escapades.

The frustrated sheriff slept during the day and patrolled at night, but being a family man he would often miss his daytime slumber and have to catch up on his sleep every few nights.

The day before Valentine's Day 1964 was a busy day for Sheriff Marshal, and he lay down at dusk for a short nap before patrolling on what he figured would be a rendezvous night for the Phantom Lovers. He fell into deep, needed sleep. His wife went to bed, leaving her tired husband on their couch.

It was 2:00 a.m. when he jerked awake, looked at his wristwatch, and hoped he had not missed an opportunity to surprise the Lovers. All he had to do was jump into his chevy and drive stealthily with his lights off to the last places the lovers had done it. As usual, his first stop was city hall to look in his office, because he was determined that his personal space, especially his desk top, would not be violated ever again.

He drove slowly through a cloudy, moonless night, barely able to make out the streets in the darkness. As he approached Main and 6th, the center of the business district, he saw two dim lights ahead in what he figured to be the center of Main. He shifted into neutral and silently coasted to a stop within twenty feet of the small flickering lights. Then he pulled the Chevy's headlight switch.

In the glare of headlights set two orange

candles and a blue, horse blanket, two empty bottles of roset, a pile of rose petals, and two, spent condoms. A note read, “A special place for a special day, good for us you didn’t come this way,” and was signed, “The Phantom Lovers. P.S. Your wife has bought you a Valentine card.”

Sheriff Marshal returned to his Chevy and grabbed his notebook and wrote an entry, “Clue #64–who was in the store when my wife bought me a Valentine card—they are all suspects.”

The sheriff’s wife said she had bought the card in Haygap and didn’t remember seeing anybody from Hanghat when she did. Under the strain of questioning she broke down and recalled that she had mentioned the card to Gigi.

Sheriff Marshal knew the trail just went to everybody’s house in town and the uplift when his wife had told the telephone operator, Gigi Malheur, who was the root of the Hanghat grapevine and who only rivaled St. Thomas as a hearer of sins and transgressions. Thomas was mute, but Gigi had job-hardened vocal chords and the soul of a reporter. For the latest gossip or news or historical updates, all one had to do was ring-up Gigi.

The sheriff’s first opportunity to confront a large group of suspects was a town meeting at city hall. He had asked for ten minutes to talk about the Phantom Lover situation. He planned to observe his audience to look for any squirming or quilt-revealing reactions such as eye aversion, as mentioned in a detective novel about a brilliant interrogator for the Los Angeles P.D.

The meeting commenced and finally it was the sheriff's turn to speak. He stood close to Wet Spot because the valiant dog was located next to the only electric outlet in the room. Sheriff Marshal plugged-in his new adjustable height, full reflector, interrogation light, and directed it out toward the audience.

His audience waited, looking at their sheriff standing next to the stuffed Wet Spot. The figure's lips had shrunk through the years, and the once friendly, stuffed dog appeared to be snarling viciously. The sheriff switched on the light.

"Good God, Marshal, shut off that damn light," several blinded people said as everybody shielded their eyes from the thousand watt glare of the "Confession Master."

Marshal hurriedly turned the light around toward the wall and Wet Spot, which, with its snarl ultra-lit by the "Confession Master," looked as if it was about to leap onto the audience. Sheriff Marshal thought that according to the literature that came with the light, somebody may have been driven to spilling their guts if only he could have grilled them for a few minutes in its glare.

Sheriff Marshal apologized, adjusted his hat, then addressed the group, "I want to ask you all if you have any ideas about the Phantom Lovers. As you know they did it in the middle of the intersection of Main and 6th, and it's getting out of hand. For all we know they're somewhere out there right now spreading one of their stolen blankets in somebody's office or kitchen or front yard. . . . And I think it's somebody that I would not suspect."

A woman said, "I thought they paid for those blankets."

A man in the audience asked, "Do you suspect anyone here tonight?"

"Of course not," lied the sheriff.

Edna Mae then said, "Didn't you just say that you think it's somebody you wouldn't suspect? Doesn't that mean you suspect everybody here?"

"No, just because I don't suspect you doesn't mean that I suspect you."

"But that's not what you just said," replied Edna.

"Well, that's not what I meant. What I'm saying is, is that it must be somebody from here that is doing it here. Wouldn't you all say so? I mean I've never noticed a strange car in town when something has gone on . . . I think I need help to solve this case, maybe the Texas Rangers."

"Marshal," said Edna, "I don't believe this fits into a category of bank robbery or whatever it would take to get the Texas Rangers out to Hanghat. Let's just all keep our eyes open and they'll eventually get caught, especially since they are getting more and more brazen like they want to get caught. Why don't you deputize the whole town so we can all be vigilantes of love? That way we can all be looking for them, and arrest them on the spot. Buck naked."

Everybody present raised their right hand and was deputized, then, after a ten minute argument about parliamentary procedures, they each grabbed the chair they came with, and went to the Queen for coffee.

One person in the meeting was stimulated when Edna mentioned the words, "bank robbery," but that one person was thinking about doing something in the vault, other than taking its contents. That person, with chair in hand, tingled with excitement, thinking about doing it in the bank vault. Naked in a bed of money. That person imagined all the town discovering them. That person imagined a crowd standing and staring at a couple in the opened vault just as they reached climax.

Sheriff Marshal returned his "Confession Master" to his office and locked the two padlocks on his door, then he locked the city hall doors and followed the crowd to the Queen.

During the discussion at the Queen, Sheriff Marshal found out that he was probably the last person in town to know about the Phantom Lover lottery. He was incensed when he heard that such a lottery existed, but he calmed down when he was reminded that no one had won it, yet, and that the current sum of more than five hundred dollars awaited the person who correctly predicted the next location of Phantom Lover activity.

The next day Sheriff Marshal handed Edna his five dollars and a sealed envelope containing his guess. He felt confident that the detective stories he had read had given him insight that would let him claim the prize money.

The following day found the sheriff

standing in the bank.

"Darn it! I should of seen this coming," said a frustrated Sheriff Marshal standing next to Moody Marlin.

The two men and the teller, Mr. Perry Riesel, were shaking their heads.

Mr. Riesel was saying, "I can't see how they got into that vault. I'm positive it was locked and the combination spun when we left yesterday."

"I saw you spin it, Perry," said Moody. "Whoever it was must have somehow had the combination."

Sheriff Marshal, his hand scratching under his hat, asked, "Who all had the combination?"

"Just me and Perry. My wife knew the old combination but only us knew the new one. Doesn't make any sense."

Sheriff Marshal peered into the vault at the pile of bills spread out on the floor, at the three empty wine bottles, at shattered wine glasses laying close to the vault's back wall.

"Three bottles," the sheriff said. "They must of been pretty damn drunk when they left here."

He turned and looked at Moody's mahogany desk where a horse blanket was spread. And all of Moody's desk articles had been swept off the desk, and they lay around on the floor.

"I'll tell you, Moody, they like to do it on your desk. I already found that out."

The sheriff continued looking around while Moody and Mr. Riesel began stacking bills and counting. The sheriff was standing, looking at the curtains on the street windows.

"Were the curtains open when you arrived this morning?" he asked.

"Yes they were. I came in first," replied Mr. Riesel.

Sheriff Marshal's attention turned to the lobby area and he said, "They like to do it where they could get caught . . . where they could be seen. Did you find anything unusual out here in front?"

Moody quit gathering bills and walked to the sheriff and looked about the area. "The pens and forms are not on the customer table," he said.

From the vault Mr. Riesel said, "Oh, yes. They're on the shelf at the teller's cage. That's where they were when I opened up."

Sheriff Marshal, having just completed a novel in which a forearm print had caught a perpetrator, moved to where the light coming through the street windows reflected to his eyes from the shiny, waxed top of the customer table. He was thinking, finger prints, when it dawned on him what he was actually seeing. There it was, a perfect set of butt-cheek prints appearing dull on the shiny wood surface.

"We've got prints," he shouted to both men. "We've got a perfect set of prints."

Mr. Riesel came from the vault, and he and Moody took turns looking from the point of view that best revealed the prints.

It was Mr. Riesel who asked, "What good are they? I don't think you'll ever get the women of Hanghat to give butt prints."

"That's right," replied Sheriff Marshal, "but the prints can tell us about how big the woman was. All I need to do is have a small and a medium and a fatter woman sit on a shiny surface to get an idea of what sized woman made these. That'll narrow my suspects."

"Who do you plan on asking, Marshal?" asked Moody. "I'd hate to have that job."

Then, Mr. Riesel asked a disturbing question, "What if they're the man's butt?"

Sheriff Marshal did get his wife to sit nude on their kitchen table, after which he measured the impressions. She balked at supplying a second set with her legs spread apart, so, figuring he had insufficient data, he abandoned the idea and simply began having a job-connected reason for doing something men naturally do anyway.

Nobody knew that only he, among all the men sitting on the corner watching all the girls go by, was on official business when he dutifully turned his head to compare and contrast a passing woman's rear with his memory of the print in the bank.

No one guessed correctly about the next outing by the Lovers. One week after the bank job the lovers were, as estimated by Sheriff Marshal, going at it in the ticket booth at the Josephine Theatre sometime around midnight Saturday. The upholstered stool showed dried stains of wine and other fluids, and the only prints were those of a left, bare foot on one side of the booth's windows, and a right, bare foot on the other side.

Sheriff Marshal secretly had a store clerk come to the booth to determine the foot size. The next day the sheriff sat at the corner of Main and 6th to watch butts and feet. There were few people out, so he drove over to the Queen, where the action was, and he watched for the right-sized butt with the right-sized feet. He pretended to read the Uplift Picayune while he kept a lookout through a small hole he had punched in the center of a page—a trick he had learned in a correspondence course from the "Famous Detective School."

CHAPTER 23

On certain mornings when driving the road from Phleville to Hanghat, the uplift could be seen in the distance as terra incognita adrift upon a cloud ocean. Two other imagination evoking views from afar were those days when low clouds would seem to reveal only the base of a towering mountain, and those days in spring sunshine when the slopes below an Elysium were green and covered with wild flowers.

Three years had passed, and the unclaimed, Phantom Lover lottery had steadily grown to more than four thousand dollars. That amount caused many of the players to worry about some kind of cheating by the other participants, and it caused some of the players to think about the possibility of snatching a used blanket and create a fake scene, then collect the prize for correctly guessing the site. At a lottery meeting it was decided to place the accrued evidence inside a locked chest inside the bank's vault. Erlene Dumas would have the key to one lock, and Sheriff Marshal would hold the key to a second lock.

It was one of the days when the rising road to the uplift, like Jack's beanstalk, disappeared into a hovering cloud. The marquee above the Josephine Theatre read, "on Wit in." It was the holiday season of 1969, and the usual weirdness had been happening in Hanghat for the past three years.

Dr. Leander Bertram was crazed from years

of attempting diagnoses by questioning Uplifters who answered in non sequiturs. He had shared his home with a succession of five dogs since his arriving in Hanghat. At the age of seventy-two, he had repeatedly warned his runt dog, Dirty Spot, against swimming in Train Lake, lest the giant catfish consume him, but the willful, adventurous young dog could not resist a daily swim after digging or jumping from the doctor's fenced yard.

Llano Bandera, the only employee of the Greater Hanghat Park Or Sidewalk Department, had come to the doctor's house to inform him that he had just seen the catfish eat the dog. Dr. Bertram, crazed upon crazed, then filled his largest hypodermic syringe with morphine, and headed for Train Lake to kill the dog-eating goddamned fish.

It was two days after Christmas when the monster finally swam from its lair to the surface for an aquatic equivalent of a walkabout.

Sitting in a rowboat and manning the oars was Llano. Dr. Bertram was seated at the bow when his "great white whale" emerged from the depths for a check of its realm's surface. The men had sat in the boat for several hours each day, waiting for the fish to show itself.

Llano excitedly pointed and shouted in Spanish, "El pescado monstruoso."

Dr. Bertram, having no Spanish, translated Llano's excited, finger-pointing words as, "Thar she blows."

He threw off the blanket he had huddled under, and he got a grip on the hypodermic full of morphine. "Row us over to him easy, we don't want to scare him under. The puppy eating son of a bitch."

The doctor then leaned over the side of the boat and reached out with the needle as they approached the fish. Suddenly, the doctor fell into the cold water. His head of bushy white hair wilted down over his neck and face.

The catfish sensed the splash and determined that whatever had made it was too big to eat, so it ignored the splashing creature and continued to sun itself.

"Keep rowing," commanded the doctor, holding onto the boat with one hand, and holding the needle in the other hand, above the water, like it was a harpoon.

The fish filled its swim bladder with air to float has high in the warm sunshine as possible. It ignored the unswallowable object floating slowly to him. Its beady little eyes appeared to be dreamily staring into the distance when Dr. Bertram injected ten cc's of morphine into the unconcerned fish.

Llano and the doctor got to shallow water where Llano helped the doctor back into the boat, and then they sat watching the catfish for the effects of what the doctor figured was a lethal dose.

After thirty minutes the catfish slowly rotated until it was belly-up, causing its naturally glum, fish-mouth frown to appear as a smile.

Three hours later about thirty people sat in their new, Christmas mazettes while they watched

Llano and Dr. Bertram struggling to get the ponderously heavy and very slippery fish onto shore, but all that the constant pulling and swishing and rolling achieved was the reviving of the creature, which began to steam about Train Lake like a submarine on surface patrol.

Someone in the crowd of sitters shouted, "I thought the damned thing was dead. Why don't we shoot it or hit it with something?"

While people offered suggestions, nobody noticed the exact moment the catfish dived out of sight.

Other than episodes of catfish calamities, parties hosted by Erlene at Fissile House, and a bit of cold weather-subdued outdoor fornication, the winter of '69-'70 was sat through by most Uplifters at home. The highschool enrollment was so low that the football squad could only field a six-man team, which played a short schedule with other small towns in Heespud and Tick counties. Both SBA retreats were closed from September through April, and on some cold wintery afternoons Hanghat could be mistaken for a freshly abandoned ghost town.

With no one else out and about, the caretaker who lived year round at the 3rd Street SBA was considered as a prime Phantom Lover suspect by the sheriff, because not only was the man seen walking to the Tasting Room every day, but he was also drinking beer, which Sheriff Marshal thought was mighty suspicious—a Baptist drinking beer. He was sure that the ten dollars he had paid for a subscription to "The Rural

Lawman" magazine was beginning to pay off, since an article in that publication had reminded him about keeping an eye out for unusual or aberrant behavior in suspects.

Elgin Giddings, the caretaker, had already discovered the sheriff's stakeout long ago when, after hearing a radio playing country music, he went from the compound and found the sheriff asleep in his car while Patsy Cline fell to pieces.

In the autumn of 1969, Sheriff Marshal LeConte's locked-up collection of horse blanket evidence included all but the fiftieth blanket, and living under that wooly sword of Damocles had driven the once model of mental health into an obsessive compulsive state caused by a vexing need to apprehend the Phantom Lovers during their last performance. If the caretaker hunch was correct, he had one last chance to retire with no unsolved cases, and, this being the only case he had ever had, keeping track of the caretaker could mean all or nothing.

His theory was that the Lovers had always wanted the thrill of being seen in flagrante delicto, and, therefore, the final horse blanket boinking would be a public affair. It was a finale he dreamed of witnessing, for testifying in court only, of course, he told himself. Yes, to watch long enough to testify meant coitus interruptus performed as an official duty. He imagined the sound of a bottle being uncorked when he pulled the Phantom Lovers apart. He only had to figure out when and where the event would transpire.

Two weeks before Christmas, the sheriff

had what he thought was a brilliant idea. He then drove to Heespud City and purchased Phantom Lover bait. The bait included two expensive bottles of the Lovers' favorite brand of wine, and two crystal, wine glasses setting in a bed of red rose petals in a deluxe applewood box. He then had the bait prominently displayed in Collage's Department Store. He felt certain that the Lovers would have to have it for a decent finale. He told the storekeepers to keep quiet, and offered a reward of fifty dollars for the name of a purchaser, and once he knew who they were, tail them and catch them in midstream, naked as jay birds. As a side benefit, he would de facto collect the lottery funds, he assured himself.

With his bait in place, Sheriff Marshal felt he could get a good night's, visions-of-sugar-plums sleep after incessant night patrols and hours spent sitting in his car in the darkness beyond the gates of the 3rd Street SBA waiting for the prime suspect to reappear and skulk through the shadows, unknowing that he was being stalked by a well-read professional detective.

However, across town one of the Phantom Lovers, sleeping alone as usual, dreamed another variation of a recurring theme: It is a moonless night when he and she spread their final blanket on a platform and disrobe under a spotlight that only falls on them. They're going at it like rabbits when applause breaks out from the entire community who had been watching from the dark. The two then have dramatic writhing climaxes in front of everyone, then run off into the bushes where they tear away matching bandana masks and escape incognito, cartwheeling on the backs of a line of galloping ponies to flee into the forests of the Argonne.

That same night, two non suspects, the hard-working Al and Gertrude, snored loudly enough to be heard outside the airstream trailer which was their home. The airstream set behind the Queen, across the parking lot. Gertrude had planted flowers and hedges and had a small lawn inside a three-foot high chain- link fence. The couple would take turns running the nerve center of Hanghat, while the other puttered about in the yard or watched TV. During busy times in the Queen, they would both be there to help the teenagers they employed.

The Queen was the hub of all public teen activity, and it was crowded every afternoon after school and all day Saturday from opening at ten a.m. to closing at ten p.m. After games and other school events, Al could sometimes talk Gertrude into remaining open till eleven, or until the crowd had gone.

It was at the Queen that nineteen year old Robert Olin Beer first began to fall for seventeen year old Pauline Dumas. Robert had graduated with the Hanghat High class of '69, and Pauline was a junior who would graduate in 1970.

It was a summer evening and Robert and Pauline were sitting in the Queen when he had for the first time noticed that Pauline had beautiful brown eyes and light brown hair and a cute figure. She was a bit skinny, but males of that era had already lost the instinct of first noticing adequate, child bearing hips, and his attention went straight for her chest and face.

Of course they had known each other since early childhood, but they had only considered each other to be part of the crowd at school, except for one fretful moment 1964 when a teacher, new in the community of sitters, didn't include enough chairs for all the participants in a cake walk. When the music stopped every walker got a seat, except Robert.

What the new teacher did not understand was that, in Hanghat, it was the last person to sit who was removed from the game each time the music stopped. Any Hanghatter could have an anxiety attack upon being without a chair when all those around him were suddenly sitting. It was the eleven year old Pauline Dumas who saw the chair-less Robert turn pale and stagger a bit. As his eyes began to roll back in his head, she jumped from her seat, guided him back to it, and sat him down. Robert had no memory of the caring moment, but Pauline did.

Soon after that 1970 Queen encounter, where the two had been so overcome with mutual infatuation, Robert, who lived two blocks from her, found himself to be regularly taking the long way home just to drive past her house.

Pauline, the only member of the Hedgehog Debate Team, had promised herself that she would be on his side, should an impromptu debate ever arise, no matter what the subject, and she fantasized that Robert and she, as a team, defeated the Phleville Philology Society.

After a third drive-by, Robert saw Pauline in her front yard, sitting in a swing suspended beneath the yard's large oak.

He stopped the pickup, and from inside hollered, "Would you like some company? I've got a while before I'm due at my job."

"That's fine," replied Pauline, and she pushed off and began swinging. "Come and swing me if you feel like it."

Robert parked and walked behind her and pushed on the ropes until Pauline said, "That's high enough. Keep me going just like you're doing."

They both felt excitement as Robert ceased pushing against the ropes and moved his hands to her waist, gently pushing her forward at the end of each back swing.

After feeling his hands on her waist several more times, she began to feel embarrassed, so she bailed out and landed laughing as she took a few steps, then turned to face Robert.

"Would you like to try it? I'll give you a start."

Robert sat in the swing, and she pulled it backward by the ropes, as high as she could lift him, and then she ran forward, pushing against the small of his back, then she dodged away and stood and watched as Robert pumped the swing until the ropes slackened and jerked at the top of his travel, then he bailed out and sailed to the ground and fell forward.

Pauline ran over to him and asked, "Are

you hurt?"

Betty Joe came onto her porch, and she said something neither Pauline nor Robert heard, as Pauline came to stand the customary, friends-only, eighteen inches from Robert as he stood up, dusted his pants, and replied, "No, golly no, it would take a lot more than a jump from a swing to hurt me."

Robert moved an intimate inch closer to her, and she backed away from him, regaining the friends-only distance of eighteen inches, from where she turned her head toward her mother on the porch. "Did you say something, Mom?" she asked.

Betty Joe replied, "Hi, Robert. Pauline we have some things to do. Will you be long?"

"Goodbye, Robert. I've gotta go," she said. "Stop anytime you want to."

She walked a few steps toward the porch, then turned to see if Robert was watching her, or if he was already going to his pickup. She was satisfied to see that he was doing both. She smiled at him, and thought how exciting it would be to have him as a boyfriend.

The two dated until Pauline's senior year when Robert asked her to marry him. He gave her an engagement ring while on his knee at table #1, just inside the entrance of the Queen. He called her the Princess of the Queen, and she vowed eternal love.

At that time she knew her love would be eternal, but was it the feeling that of all of the close talking, always sitting, uplift mothers of none, not knowing the powerful DNA persuader dwelling in them would some day wail like a silent Siren beckoning them away from the father of their first born, placing a pail in their hands, and sending them wandering the uplift in search of different stuff from which babies are made. Pauline meant every word she said.

CHAPTER 24

Hamlin Paducha was the owner of Hamlin's Handy Home Construction. Hamlin had three employees who helped him repair damage from lightning strikes and termites. The last new house to be added to the uplift was completed shortly after the appearance of the secret building's associated tract homes on Cutoff Blvd. and Project Way. Hamlin's company had never had the opportunity to build a new home.

With no new housing, it was to relative's homes and the tract homes that Uplifters returned after having had little success in adapting to big city jobs where one was expected to stand all day and maintain an uncomfortable, greater than twenty-four inches, distance from customers. And, needless to say, many unadaptable Uplifters didn't excel in jobs where speech was used to communicate precise instructions, or any other information.

However, some Uplifters had settled into a specialized niche in which they did very well. These descendants of FL had the rare ability to decipher and rewrite product assembly instructions that had already been translated into unintelligible English by somebody in the orient.

Young, college graduate Avec Mouvoir gained immediate fame in the world of imports when he deciphered the mysterious, "Please finger the way of the prominent rodded nut so do ceases the tiger from leaping," as meaning, "Tighten the nut while holding the spring in place."

Gradually all the tract homes were occupied. The residents planted so many bushes and trees and vines to cover the neighborhood's pole-mounted, lightning rods, that the area became known as the Jungle, and the foliage obscured houses, the Jungalows. Then the birth control pill came to Hanghat and many children remained sibling-less, but the dense foliage remained necessary as sanctums to satisfy the lust component of the FL gene.

Hamlin Paducha finally got the job of building a complete house when Florence Ficher, who was baking and jumping in her kitchen at the time, had lightning strike her house and set it afire. When it was over, the house was gone.

Hamlin Paducha began rebuilding the house from the ground, up. He had talked Florence into having her new house built upon a concrete slab foundation, and that was Florence's undoing. Florence, widowed for five years, had made a living from two hundred dollars social security per month, plus an income from her delicious pudding cakes. Part of the secret to her cakes was that she used no pudding. Another secret was how she managed to achieve a cheesecake-like texture without using cheese.

Edna and Erlene were among Florence's regular customers. So was the current owner of the Bouquet Bakery, Ames Coryell, who would purchase the pudding cakes, not only because they were a joy to eat, but also to analyze them, attempting to learn their secrets and bake his own.

Ames was buying two pudding cakes a week, and he had become obsessed with determining the recipe. He was distraught after Florence's production ceased, and he would regularly drive past the construction of her new home to observe the progress, stopping occasionally to ask Hamlin when the house would be completed. Ames had already offered the Widow Ficher a job as baker at the Bouquet, as well as a sum of money for her recipe, but the stubborn woman refused his offers and told him that she would take the recipe to her grave.

The secrets to Florence's cakes were not only the ingredients, but also included the act of jumping up and down on the floor in front of the oven at a critical time to get the rising cake to fall. If the baking cake collapsed at the exact moment of increasing doneness, the result was Widow Ficher's Famous Puddin' Cake. Otherwise, it was a gooey mess, or, too cooked to collapse, it was just another fluffy cake like those sold at the Bouquet Bakery.

In her new house she began baking her first new batch of pudding cakes, but, jump as she might, the cakes would not fall. The concrete floor was too solid to vibrate. Her old house had wooden floors that shook when just walking across them.

Florence had spent the morning jumping, but not one cake had responded, and she had four, light, fluffy failures setting on her kitchen table. Florence was befuddled and feeling dizzy from the activity.

Coming to buy a cake, were two puddin' cake connoisseurs who had barely managed to make it through the cake-less weeks since Florence's production had been interrupted. Edna Mae and Erlene Louise arrived at Florence's new front door and smelled a burning cake. They went into the kitchen and found Florence half dead on the floor in front of her new range.

"Just let me get my breath," said Florence as she raised her head. "Help me up to a chair."

"What's been going on, Florence?" asked Edna. "Did you have an attack or a stroke or something?"

Edna helped her into a kitchen chair, and Erlene turned off the oven and opened the back door to air-out the smokey room.

Erlene said, "We'd best take her to the doctor. Don't you think so?"

Florence answered, "I ain't had no attack or nothin'. I'm just winded. I've been jumpin' up and down all morning baking, an' I can't get one crumby cake to puddinize right. It must be the new stove. . . . I sorely miss my ole one that burned up."

Erlene said, "You see, Edna, I told you I'd come over and caught her jumping in front of her stove, and the whole house was shaking."

Florence abruptly stood up, then fell back into her chair. "That's it," she declared. "My old house shook better'an this new one. Y'all haven't told anyone you saw me jumpin', have you? Please don't. It's been my secret for many a year. The Bouquet has offered me money for my recipe, an' I've had to shut my doors an' keep a lookout for Ames Coryell who is determined to steal my recipe. Why, I've seen him sneakin' around, an' I've been told he's workin' on a recipe of his own. He buys two cakes a week, an' sends his helpers, like that would fool me."

Erlene told her, "I didn't know why you were jumping. I thought you might be happy or having a fit of some kind, but I never thought it had anything to do with baking your cakes. My lips are sealed. Aren't yours, Edna?"

"Well, of course they are. I'll tell you Florence, these are cement floors and they won't shake or move at all."

"I'm ruined then," lamented Florence. "Half my livin' is my cakes, an' if I can't jump 'em down . . . well, I'm done. I'll have to move somewhere into a shaky house, or go broke."

"I've got a wild idea, girls," said Edna. "Let's put the stove up on a rickety platform that sticks out far enough to jump on, and not tell anybody why it's being done, so your baking secret can stay that way, Florence."

Hamlin Paducha had no idea why he was called to put a poorly built, springy wood, raised floor under Florence's kitchen stove. If it had been only the old widow's wish, he would have probably refused to do such a crazy thing, but Edna Dumas herself had told him to do it; to build it where it would shake just like the old floor, but wouldn't break if somebody was to jump on it regularly.

On the first day after the platform was

ready, Erlene and Edna waited at the kitchen table with Florence while a first attempt baked.

After a while Florence stood up, saying, “Smell that? See how the smell just changed from batter to a hint of a cake baking? That means it’s almost time.”

She gingerly stepped onto the platform, which extended three feet in front of the stove, cracked opened the oven door, and sniffed the hot, rising aroma.

“Not just yet,” whispered the mistress of the perfect pudding cake.

Another sniff test and the baker said, “Here goes.”

She bent her knees to gather energy for a decisive first jump, then her feet lifted from the floor and she began hopping in place.

Erlene began to whistle the tune to the “Irish Washerwoman.” Edna joined in. Florence broke into a heel-and-toe, then a brief Appalachian clog dance followed by a few jitterbug steps and ending with some Charleston, knee flaps.

“It feels just like the ole floor,” she panted. “I think it’s goin’ to work.”

Twelve minutes after the applause ended, the dancing baker removed a perfectly fallen masterpiece from the oven, and set it on a cooling rack.

“I think it’s my best ever,” said the grateful baker, “and I want y’all to take it home an’ enjoy it.”

CHAPTER 25

Fissile House had needed some repairs and paint for the last few years, but nobody in the uplift was doing very well financially. Edna's previous entrepreneurial escapades, along with some investment failures, had left the Fissile trust low on cash, but still owning land on the uplift.

Ten years back they did have Hamlin's Handy Home Services do some work at the mansion, including putting a layer of asphalt shingles over the roof's original, many times repaired, wooden shingles, and having the downstairs rooms carpeted with fashionable, olive green shag rug. In 1963, Hamlin had put another layer of asphalt shingles over the hail-damaged older ones, and he added another layer of the more fashionable orange shag over the olive green shag.

Hamlin assured his customers that covering the old with the new was a common installation practice that added insulation to the house.

After a Fissile trust payment was made to Edna and Erlene early in 1966, they had the even more fashionable gold color of shag installed, and, as was his custom, Hamlin installed it over the outdated orange shag which Erlene called, jejune, without knowing the meaning of the word or how it had come to her vocabulary. Edna, who had always thought the orange shag was a mistake, even when first seeing it in place, agreed with her sister's word for it, assuming that jejune meant something unacceptable.

Erlene and Edna finally arrived at Fissile

House with the still warm, Widow Ficher's Famous Puddin' Cake setting in the back seat of their 1952 dodge. The old car was having trouble going into a forward gear, and Edna, who did all the driving, had to back up the last quarter mile to the house.

"You get the cake, Erlene, and I'm going to call Cheval's to see if they can look at Hazel and see if they can fix her before she's broken down completely, and we're walking."

Edna went on into the house. She was on the phone when Erlene entered carrying the cake. Erlene was doing the necessary high step which had to be done when walking over the three spongy, shoe grabbing layers of shag over an extra thick foam pad. She was passing the couch, her knees were pumping, but, still, her left shoe became shag-bound and she tripped and fell onto the couch, managing to spin so that she landed back first, saving the cake, which had remained on its platter.

"Thank God," Erlene said, exhaling the words. She yelled out to Edna, "I just saved the cake."

Edna was on the phone to Cheval's service station and she had not seen the almost calamitous mishap.

She hung up and turned toward Erlene who was looking at the various old stains on the gold shag where everything from coffee, to full dinner plates, had left the hands of tumbling, shag victims.

Erlene adamantly said, "We've got to have

something done about this rug . . . this shagmire. I just barely saved the cake. I'm tired of having to wade around the house. Lifting our knees up so high has become such a habit that I caught myself walking around the general store like I was stomping grapes, and I got funny looks from folks. I feel sure this rug has become jejuned."

"Well, you know we'll have to keep wading until that money comes from the fund . . . and that'll be another three months. I'm heading down to Cheval's. They said they'll check the transmission and see about getting us in gear, but first let's get that cake to the kitchen and have a slice. I'm too puddin' cake deprived to go any further."

Edna backed out to Fissile Lane and backed toward Main Street. There, she made a left and backed up Main all the way to the service station at 10th.

She was being driven back to Fissile House in the station's wrecker when the town fire alarm sounded from city hall.

City hall itself was on fire, and Edna and the wrecker arrived before any of the members of the volunteer fire department.

Sheriff Marshal was carrying things from the burning building, and Edna saw him enter the building again just as they drove up.

The sheriff rushed in and out until it was too hot and smoky to return. He had managed to save important things like his Phantom Lover folders and maps, three old file cabinets of Hanghat records, a couple-dozen chairs, and the brave Wet Spot, before intense heat forced everybody to sit at a distance and watch the old wood, city hall burn to the ground.

Sheriff Marshal kept the cause of the fire to himself, since it would be to embarrassing to admit it started because he had placed the Confession Master interrogation light too close to a Playboy centerfold pinned to a wall. He had been practice grilling his smiling, seminude suspect when he had to go pee. He was sure that she was about to breakdown and tell all. As he zipped up, he thought he smelled something burning, but he continued to look in the mirror, adjusting his new white, ten gallon, Ranger model hat, so he would look his best when the guilty, hot centerfold divulged her lover's name.

The temporary replacement, city hall was a long, long trailer of 1950's style with a bay window in the front. Snarling more than ever, Wet Spot was placed on the shelf of the bay window. Facing the outside, Wet Spot looked like a menacing figurehead above a trailer hitch bowsprit.

The temporary city hall was temporarily parked at the corner of Front and 6th streets. Sheriff Marshal set up his office in the trailer's back bedroom, and the front of the trailer was used for city business.

Edna and Erlene were in the trailer refiling old city papers when Erlene came across a handwritten page about the founding of Hanghat.

"Edna, look at this, it says that Hanghat was founded on May 14, 1861, and the person who wrote this letter, a Mrs. Agnes Roue, was there."

She looked over Erlene's shoulder and they read together: ". . . and when Eccrine Fissile came to consciousness we were gathered around him, and Mme. Fissile said to him that he was in Hanghat, Texas."

"That's peculiar," said Edna, "the Heespud County records say that our town was founded in 1872, and there was only farms here on the uplift till then."

Erlene said, "If this is true, then we missed our centennial celebration by ten years so far."

The lawn outside the city hall trailer was packed on a September 1970 afternoon when Hanghat voted to hold a "Centennial Plus Ten" celebration on May 14, 1971. Festivities were to include a gala float parade with folks wearing 1861 attire, a carnival at the fair grounds, and a baked-goods sale.

Dr. Bertram, still pissed at the puppy gulping catfish, warned the gathering that the Train Lake monster had grown large enough to swallow a small adult, then he mentioned having read about some catfish that walked on land.

The assembly looked at each other and realized they were all small adults, so a catfish catching contest was added to the planned festivities, and until it was caught, several people said a fence should be erected around Train Lake to contain the possibly amphibious, people eating beast lest it walk into somebody's bedroom for a late night snack.

CHAPTER 26

Hazel needed a new transmission, and there was no money for one. So, Edna's last instructions to Knox, the mechanic at Cheval's, was to get her car fixed so that, at least, she could drive it around in Hanghat.

Knox was an innovative jury-rigger known for keeping vehicles running when they would otherwise have been junked if it was not for his genius at accomplishing cheap, unconventional repairs.

Edna returned to Cheval's to find that Knox had indeed made Hazel roadworthy, but only in the basic sense of the word. He had tied headlights on the trunk lid, brake lights on the front fenders, and windshield wipers on the rear window. The required electrical wiring was duct-taped along the outside of the car.

Knox watched proudly as Edna inspected Hazel, but before her amazement let her speak, Knox said, "She still won't go into any gear but reverse, but since you only use her to mostly come and go from your house, and that's little over a mile, I figured all this out for only twenty-five dollars, and you're just borrowing the lights until the transmission is fixed, and that's a savin's right there. How's she look?"

"It'll have to do me," replied Edna. Then thinking she may have hurt Knox's feelings with the disgusted tone of her voice, she added cheerfully, "I mean, I think it's the work of a master at getting a job done when nobody else could have even thought of such a thing."

"Thank you, Mrs. Dumas, "It was all I could think of. I done what you told me. I hope twenty-five isn't too much. I had to buy the wiper motors but I can reuse the wires and all."

"It's a wonderful job, Knox. More than I expected could be done for the price."

Edna paid, then backed out and across Main, staying on 10th, backing east to Front Street so she could avoid traffic until she was more practiced at driving backward. As she drove, she thought about the times she had shared with the old car, and she recalled the most memorable event ever to occur in Hazel. That single event was the main reason she had kept the car for so long.

It happened when Hazel was brand new in 1952 and had less than a hundred miles on her. Edna was coming to town daily in the shiny new car, then, on one rainy afternoon at the general store, the clerk asked her if she could drop off the groceries for Au Revoir at his bunker. The clerk, a Mr. Mutin, had said that his lumbago was bothering him, and, since the delivery boy had been out sick for two days, Au Revoir could be out of food. He reminded Edna that the unlucky recluse had no refrigerator, and only ate raw food, baked goods, and cold cuts, because he was wary of having anything lit in his fortress, including a cooking fire.

She loaded two boxes of groceries into the trunk and drove to the bunker. There she had to sit inside the car while it rained too hard to get out without being soaked.

Au Revoir saw her waiting, and in a daring, foolhardy move, the unlucky man, venturing a sizzling death by lightning, opened his front door, sloshed to the car, and tapped on the passenger window.

Just then the rain-filled air flashed, and a thunderclap shook the new dodge. Edna, fearful for Au Revoir's safety, frantically motioned for him to get in, which the wet and frightened man quickly did after glancing at the thirty foot distance he would have to sprint across to regain the safety of his bunker.

Edna was a twenty-nine year old quasi-virgin when the wet and handsome twenty-three year old Au Revoir shut the car door. The rain continued for the hour they talked, then they were kissing, then Edna was in the back seat of her new car with one foot against the back window and the other over the back of the passenger seat.

Just before she temporarily lost her mind to ecstasy, she heard her mother's admonition repeated to her when a teenager: "Dress down and panties up, and your parasol ready for a defensive blow." But, she was too busy to search for a parasol, or panties.

She showed up with groceries at Au Revoir's door three more times in the following weeks, but, even after honking the horn and waiting, he never came out or even appeared at his door. She would drive by the next day after each late afternoon delivery to find that the groceries were gone, so she assumed that he didn't want to see her, anymore.

What she didn't know was that on the three subsequent attempts to be with her again, he was first, unconscious from hitting his head on a beam in a mad dash to get to the door and open it upon hearing the sound of her horn, then second, was almost comatose from an allergic reaction to a wasp sting while cleaning his living space so he could invite her in, and thirdly, during her final try at union, he had been stuck under his bed for several hours after crawling under it during a search for clean underwear. He had worked himself free and opened his door just in time to see the '52 dodge disappear around the corner.

Since that last visit in 1952, broken hearted and feeling rebuked, she had never returned to the bunker, but, whenever she drove past Au Revoir's, she would glance down at the back seat and vividly remember their interlude and what son-of-a-bitches men could be.

Driving backwards and having to look at the back seat had brought back those memories. "Men are pains in the ass," she declared, "aren't they, Hazel?" She rubbed her neck and mumbled to herself, so Hazel wouldn't hear and be offended, "And driving twisted around like this is a pain in the neck."

As it came to be, the Fissile fortune fizzled when a trustee absconded with the liquid assets. With an untidy sum of money available in Agneau Bank & Real Estate, the Dumas sisters found themselves to be on a strict budget without the money to replace the transmission in Hazel. Uplifters soon became accustomed to seeing the car backing down the streets.

The three sister's mother, Genevieve, had inherited Fissile's Wine Company and the Tasting Room, but, like the other businesses in Hanghat, they were not very profitable, and only did a mediocre volume of business, even when the two SBA's were open. Genevieve still owned Collage Department Store, and she insisted upon sharing its meager profits equally with her daughters.

Edward Dumas had died in 1968 leaving Genevieve with farm debts and a second mortgage, but the seventy year old Genevieve, who was yet beautiful and looked twenty years younger, was still pitching hay to her cows and making cheese. Her hair was sun-streaked and her fair skin was tanned. She would tell her visiting daughters to mind their own business when they told her to slow down and let someone else do the farm's heavy work.

Jeanette at 98 years was yet capable of gardening and getting around on her on. She was still sharing her house with Betty Joe and Pauline. Jeanette had inherited the Hanghat General Store which yielded her a moderate income.

Betty Joe had been working for the Uplift Picayune since her return to Hanghat in 1953. Since her sophomore year at Hanghat High, Pauline had worked part time behind the sales counter in the Bouquet Bakery. She enjoyed the job and the aromas. The only unpleasant thing about her job was the fit her boss, Ames Coryell, would have after each failure at replicating a Widow Ficher's Famous Puddin' Cake.

Whenever a customer was in the store, Pauline would turn red-faced with embarrassment when Ames would be heard shouting in the back of the store, "What's that old battle-axe's secret?" The question was often accompanied by the sounds of a loaded cake pan hitting a wall.

CHAPTER 27

Robert Olin Beer and Pauline did not have a

tumultuous relationship. Sure, there were times when each would have passing fears that the other would not love them forever, and there were times when each felt jealous of any attention to the other by somebody who could be imagined as a possible rival.

Robert had never realized how many boys knew Pauline. Before Cupid shot him in the butt, he couldn't recall any good looking boy ever talking to her. Now, in his eyes, they circled about her like wolves. He made sure that the word was quickly spread when he began going steady with the girl he now believed to be the most desired young woman on the uplift, and he only relaxed after he gave her the engagement ring, at which time he told himself how silly he had been for thinking her love was something to be easily stolen away by another.

Pauline had suffered the same feelings when cute girls had approached or even smiled at Robert, but, after a long talk with her mother, she had decided the feelings were normal when so much affection was involved. The two lovers felt safe in the other's arms and never were given any reason to experience any wariness, except during those capricious fancies of apprehension peculiar to the human condition of being in love.

Each had sexual fantasies in which there were two of the other, but neither would know of that betrayal until one would first admit it years in the future.

The couple would spoon at lover's point overlooking the Bratity. People heard Robert call

Pauline, Kitten, Sugar, Cuddles, and Princess, until he finally settled on, Sweetness. Sweetness called Robert, Honey, Sugar, and Bobo, until sticking with Sweetheart. Customers at the Queen stayed away from the two cooing turtle-doves at the back corner table lest they become trapped in the vortex of hearts swirling about them.

Robert was working at DeBois Lumber & Hardware when the Blizzard of '71 hit. It was the worst disaster ever to hit the uplift. A heavy, wet snow began to fall at eight in the morning on a January day. By noon about nine inches had accumulated on the rooftops of every structure. Robert was alone in the store, preparing to call it a day, when he heard a lumber shed collapse.

He ran out to the flattened shed and realized immediately that the weight of the snow had brought it down. He looked out past the lumberyard to the houses along East Street. He saw every roof laden with snow, and snow was falling so heavy as to obscure the houses along 6th Street on the other side of the burned down city hall.

He called the fire chief, Brandon Charbon, and alerted him as to the possible collapse of every house in town, if it kept snowing.

Chief Charbon informed him that his chicken coop had just caved in, and he said that an effort must be made to inform the town that the snow must be removed from roofs as quickly as possible. Chief Charbon initiated the phone tree and soon men were out removing snow from housetops.

It was too late for the homes that had been re-roofed one time too many by the lazy Hamlin Paducha's Hamlin's Handy Home Construction. Robert heard the house at 905 East Street as the rafters supporting four layers of asphalt shingles gave way and thudded down onto the walls .

He ran to the house and found the Dessous family all standing in their front yard.

Mr. Dessous was declaiming, "I told that idiot, Hamlin, that the roof would fall in with all those shingles. The idiot said the roof could support a car. He guaranteed it. The idiot . . . where's my dog and the cats? Here Slugger Spot. Where are you, boy?"

It dawned upon Robert that Pauline was at home in a house that had no telling how many layers of roofing, and he raced to the lumber yard. He threw a load of long two-by-fours into his pickup and drove through the storm, sliding and spinning down 6th, past the church, and across the West Side Street bridge over Parish Creek. As he turned right on 8th, he could see the house still standing.

Betty Joe was squirting water onto the roof but it wasn't having much effect at snow removal. She had already perceived the danger when the house had begun to creak under the load, and she had evacuated Pauline and Jeanette, who was making a snowman and having trouble lifting its head onto its torso.

Robert quickly lifted the snowman's head into place, grabbed a handful of two-by-fours, and rushed into the house. He told the women that he was bracing the rafters, and to keep out.

The Dumas women were never known to stand back from anything, especially when a request, to do so, sounded anything like an order, so Robert found Betty Joe at his side holding a saw, just as he realized that he had forgotten to bring one.

Soon, the rafters were braced to walls, and ceilings were braced to the floor, and the house was saved.

All throughout the day, roofs that could not be shoveled or braced in time could be heard crashing down. Some roofs just sagged, and some pushed out walls, collapsing the entire house. By late afternoon, the temperature had climbed above freezing and much of the snow had melted away. When it was over, Hanghat had lost eleven houses and fifty roofs. Hamlin Paducha was last seen driving out of town before anyone could shoot him.

The road out to Genevieve's farm was impassable during the storm, so she had no help with the snow. Her house did have attic rooms which had ceilings that were also rafters.

She had opened the stairway door and kept a fire in the wood stoves in the kitchen and the parlor. All was going well. The heat rising into the attic rooms was melting the snow on the roof. Genevieve was busy feeding the two stoves when the roof to the wood shed collapsed, and she had to begin searching for fuel.

She broke off an armful of branches and carried them into the house. She stopped by the stove in the kitchen, then realized she had to take the long branches back onto the porch, and cut them in two. When she turned around she didn't see that the longest stick she carried had ripped into the wallpaper, and that as she stepped toward the porch, the stick pulled a strip of wallpaper down onto the stovepipe.

She was on the porch cutting sticks when she discovered that her kitchen wall was on fire. The house burned down and Genevieve found herself living at Fissile House with her two oldest daughters until she could rebuild.

Genevieve had already learned to keep her knees high when walking across the three layers of shag carpet, and she fell onto the couch or into a chair much less often than Erlene, who had for some personal reason quit lifting her knees at all. She just shuffled through the shag while swearing that if that no good Hamlin was still around, she would hold a shotgun on him till he pulled that damned shag up with his teeth and ate it. Fissile House, with a roof built of timbers, had no trouble supporting the snow, and the old, but well-built house, had survived unharmed.

Robert replaced Hamlin as the local roofer and went into business as Robert's Roof Removal & Replacement. He hired Hamlin's old crew because they had been heard for years to say that their boss didn't know what he was doing. Robert said that post snowstorm Hanghat was to be a town of one layer roofs.

The big Centennial Plus Ten celebration approached while roofs were being torn off and put on, while Phantom Lovers schemed their finale, and an unsuspecting, self-assured catfish fearlessly sunned in Train Lake while listening for swallowable splashes.

CHAPTER 28

Robert Beer was rebuilding houses and roofs twelve hours a day, six days a week. Pauline was bringing him lunch and spending that hour with him. It was the only time they could share when Robert was not exhausted. On Sundays the two attended Catheran services and took communion with the tasty, innovative, cross-shaped wafers designed by Reverend Beer, and baked by Widow Ficher, as she was then called, at her request, thinking it would help her pudding cake business.

Florence had also asked to be referred to as the, Famous Widow Ficher, when her cakes were being discussed out of her presence, or when she was being introduced to the Betty Crocker representatives if they showed up in town. At a town meeting she had revealed that she had invited Mrs. Crocker to come and taste the puddin' cakes. She had looked directly at Ames Coryell when she said that Betty Crocker would probably offer her a million dollars for her secret recipe as soon as she got into town.

During the last Chinese New Year, Widow Ficher had folded the arms of the wafers to hold fortunes with such predictions as, "Jesus will love you even after Saturday night," and "Hell awaits those who spit too much," and "Go forth and sin rarely." She made about ten dozen of the folded fortune crosses which were such a success that she gave Reverend Beer a package of a dozen, and she told him to send it to the Catheran World Headquarters. She expected a request for a large order, but the reverend told her it probably wouldn't happen.

It was after services, one Sunday in mid February, when Robert and Pauline were approached by Mr. and Mrs. Gunter Argyle who bred dogs which were a cross between Chihuahuas and greyhounds, which they called Greyhuahuas.

They explained that they had finally achieved success in breeding a dog with a Chihuahua torso and head, and long, greyhound legs, and, with that success, they were moving to Florida to race them and make their fortune.

They were selling their house at West Street and 11th, and, because their roof had been damaged and their garage collapsed during the blizzard, they would sell the house for one third its value.

Robert and Pauline bought the house, and Moody Marlin was happy to carry a mortgage for the engaged couple, including the funds to restore the property.

The two worked at their new home every Sunday after church, and, by April's end, they had removed the kennels and all the debris from the wrecked garage, and they had built a new roof for the house. Robert was amazed and pleased with Pauline's ability to do hard work and the pleasure she took in making a home. She would work until evening if he had not insisted on stopping before they were stepping on nails or hammering their thumbs in the dark.

The town elected a committee in February to organize the May 14 events. Dr. Bertram, after persistently insisting, was chosen as committee head just to shut him up. He was only concerned about including a contest to catch the giant, pet-eating catfish, and that was all he talked about at every ensuing committee meeting. He would call the group to order, then ask for the last catfish minutes to be read.

Finally, the members began meeting in secret to avoid his inevitable interruption of each meeting with a warning about how someday the damned fish could swallow somebody important if they didn't catch the damned thing. They had agreed that the doctor had grown senile, and that he probably wouldn't remember if they told him that he had quit his position and had handed over the gavel to Edna, after the committee had voted to make the catfish catching event begin at six a.m. and continue until the fish was caught and filleted and fried.

Their ploy worked especially well because, between meetings, the city hall trailer had been moved from Front and 6th, to the corner of Front and 10th, after the temporary septic system had overflowed.

Dr. Bertram, on the night of the meeting, had gone to the old location and had found a vacant lot. He returned to his house and checked his calendar where he had written, "Next meeting," in the second blank square after the one containing a 28.

"Hell," he muttered, "February the thirtieth

is days away. City hall's gone till then. I'll go back when it's back . . . and look at this. The calendar idiots forgot to number the last two squares." He penciled-in a 29 and a 30 in the blanks, looked at his work, and wondered who he could write to complain about the printer's omission of the two days.

Patients had stopped going to Dr. Bertram six months before, when it was suggested that he retire from practice after an examination of a pregnant Mrs. Avril Griot, during which he assured her that she would have had great difficulty delivering if her penis hadn't fallen off.

At the new city hall, trailer location, it was decided that a carnival be invited to town for the event, and that a parade would go down Main and wind up at the carnival at the fair grounds. Widow Ficher and others could make some money by selling cakes and pies, and the profits from snack and beverage sales would add to the fund to build a new city hall. All this was quickly achieved without the presence of the doctor, who was at home that evening, thinking it was not February 30, yet.

Betty Joe accepted the task of finding a carnival that would travel to Hanghat on short notice. She made a phone call to some circus friends, and one mentioned that a troupe had just formed and was looking for engagements. Betty Joe then called the Blue Carnival, and a Mr. Blue answered the phone.

Betty Joe gave him the particulars, and he began to give her a dazzling, carny spiel until she interrupted, and, speaking the vernacular, told him that she had worked in the business for years. Betty Joe told him that if the show had elephants, then please do not bring them. Mr. Blue said that the only animals were the pony ride and three clowns, then he laughed at his joke before mentioning that his main attraction was a fifty foot Ferris wheel lit with flashing blue and white lights.

The 3rd Street SBA caretaker informed Hanghat that the SBA would be holding a week-long special session which would be going on during the centennial festivities. The SBA was going to be working in their gardens in an event they were calling, "Return To The Garden."

The 11th Street SBA heard about the scheduled garden party, and, not to be outdone by any dreadful and heretical Bralm's Second Synoders, decided to hold a special garden party of their own; one-upping them by planning a biblical extravaganza titled, "Return to the Garden of Eden." Then, for a coup de gras, the Bralm's First Synoders requested the services of a Baptist family of actors renowned for portrayals of Bible stories. The Johnson family, known as the Parableers, jumped at a chance to perform, and said that they would furnish an inflatable apple tree and a ten foot inflatable serpent.

Preparations were also being made by the Phantom Lovers who, conspiring late at night, had conceived a brilliant plan that would allow them to copulate nude in full view of the Centennial Plus 10 crowd, conceal their identities by wearing Lone Ranger masks, and escape into the crowd after quickly dressing and unmasking.

April 1, 1971 was fittingly the day on which all plans had been completed. Mr. Blue and his wife, Facile, now with the show name, Azure, and the carnival's cast of forty-three performers and employees had all been taking doses of silver solution long enough to be visibly blue of skin, and several women in the troupe were fighting over the right to be called Indigo.

Dr. Bertram's waking moments were only coherent when he had thoughts of the catfish catching contest, and every day he re-circled his calendar's May 14. The Phantom Lovers were as smug as the Bralm's First Synoders. Widow Ficher had ordered two, seventy pound bags of flour, and she was doing squats to build up her hopping endurance.

Sheriff Marshal had also been laying plans. He had given little thought to crowd control or directing traffic or parking. He only pondered the probable and most likely scenario expected from his chosen adversaries, and, whenever he doubted his conclusion, he would shut his mind to any other possibility. After all, he had read more than 200 mystery novels, and he was sure of his grasp of the criminal mind. He knew what the two culprits would do, and he was to be in position with a camera, two sheets to cover their nakedness from the innocent eyes of children, and two sets of handcuffs. May 14 was going to be his big day. His sealed entry in the Lover Lottery had included the date as well as the expected location.

Moody Marlin and family were to be out of

town from the third week of April until the day before the celebration.

CHAPTER 29

On May the second, a crew of men and machines arrived and began clearing the northeast corner lot at Main and 3rd. Within two hours of starting work, most of the town knew about it.

The property had been for sale for so long that the metal "FOR SALE" sign had fallen over and rusted to illegibility. The property belonged to the Fissile estate, and the family wondered what the lot had sold for and what was going to be built there, but the Marlins were somewhere on the road visiting national parks, and the workers said they couldn't say.

By the eighth of May the lot had been paved, and a concrete foundation awaited its superstructure. Then, on May 11 a prefabbed building, resembling a Daisy Queen, or some other drive-in style building, occupied the foundation. Upon being questioned, the crew that installed it said that the basic kit they erected could be one of many different drive-through businesses. They didn't respond when asked if it was a Queen or a King or a Freeze or a Frost or a Maid, and only replied that the sign would arrive and be erected in a day, or so, and the local paper should be running an ad for the grand opening.

Al and Gertrude were not happy to see a new drive-in food business going up in Hanghat. They made a comfortable living as the only such establishment in town, so they called Daisy Queen headquarters to find out what was happening. On the phone they were assured that Hanghat was not receiving a second Queen, but Haygap was, and Daisy Queen headquarters had no idea what brand of drive-in was being built in Hanghat, and that, maybe, it was a drive-in cleaners or something else.

The Samsons went to the new building and peered in the plate glass windows, but the building's furnishings were not installed; it was just an empty shell, complete on the outside except for a sign to indicate the nature of the business. Al and Gertrude eyed the drive-through window with suspicion. It looked remarkably similar to theirs.

On that same day Betty Joe had gone to Widow Ficher's to see how many cakes she had made and to discuss how the cakes were to be transported to a sales area. Betty Joe found only a dozen puddin' cakes and the widow prostrate on the sofa.

"My false teeth are somewhere in the kitchen floor," she told Betty Joe, "an' I think I've jumped too much an shook an innard out of place."

Betty Joe felt the widow's brow beneath the widow's peak and declared, "You do have a fever."

"I'm feelin' worse an' worse an' I got all my money put in flour an' ingredients for a passel of jump cakes. I gotta get outa this sofa."

Mrs. Ficher tried to rise, but she fell back and moaned, "I think I'm jumped-out. Call my husband an' tell him to look behind the picture in the hall an' get my cake recipe an' finish bakin' for me. Can you do that, Betty? An' keep my recipe safe. Watch that man from that donut shop, what's his name. Coryell. He wants to beat Mrs. Crocker to my recipe."

"Let's take care of you first, then I'll see about your cakes."

Betty Joe gathered the widow's teeth and the widow. She put Widow Ficher in the back seat of her car, then she returned to the house for a pillow and blanket. She knew there was only one place she could take the jumped-out baker, and she headed for the county hospital in Heespud City.

After helping to admit Mrs. Ficher, she called Fissile House and informed Erlene where they were. She told Erlene, "Get Edna. Go over to the widow's and get the puddin' cake recipe out from behind the picture hanging in the hall, and bake at least four dozen more cakes. Florence has all her money tied up in flour. She's bought two big sacks of it. And, she's worried about her recipe becoming known."

By six p.m. that same day, a sign had been bolted into place at the new drive-in. It was checked to make sure it lit up properly, then the installers departed, inadvertently leaving a light timer turned on which would light the sign at seven p.m. A hard rain began to fall as the installers drove out of town. Most everybody was at home and there was no traffic on Main Street.

Earlier, Edna and Erlene had backed-up over to Mrs. Ficher's, found the recipe, and backed-up the ingredients and baking pans back to

Fissile House. They were preparing to bake an experimental first puddin' cake when Pauline phoned and asked if Edna could give Jeanette a ride to the drug store for something that Jeanette did not know the name of, or what it was for, but knew what the bottle looked like when she saw it.

Edna told Erlene, "I'm going to take Jeanette to the drug store, and for God's sake don't do fancy jumping and break a leg until I get back."

Edna then stood in front of the range and did a test jump. She heard the oven racks vibrate and said, "I think one person can make them fall right. Give it a try and if it doesn't fall, then we'll jump together when I'm back."

The rain had let up, and she had Hazel's wipers set on slow when she stopped in front of Jeanette's house. She got out and opened the car door for Jeanette, who had been waiting on her porch. The ninety-nine year old woman got in, and Edna shut the door behind her, being careful in the dim light not to shut it on a brittle finger or some other dangling or sagging, body part, and have something fall off into the street.

The rain began falling in torrents as she carefully backed along. The wipers couldn't keep the rear windows clear, even on the fastest setting. The road filled with water and it was impossible to see where to steer, especially having to look out the rear window. After a few turns to avoid flooded intersections, Edna didn't know what street she was on.

It was getting darker and the rain was intensifying when the sign at the second Daisy

Queen lit up promptly at seven p.m. Edna, who had not had any idea what part of town she was backing through, was relieved to see the brightly lit sign and know exactly where she was, even though she had thought she was at the other end of town.

She rounded the corner and pulled into the back parking lot, expecting to see Al and Gertrude's trailer, but was shocked to see nothing except an object setting atop a small, square, brick building at the edge of a wooded area.

"Would you look at that," she slowly said while astonished. "What in the hell is going on here?"

Jeanette was staring blankly at the faintly lit scene when a series of lightning flashes burned away cobwebs grown over nestled memories. She intently gazed at the structure as the lightning lit the scene again, exposing in her mind an imagined x-ray picture of the contents of the brick enclosure.

Jeanette shouted, "That's the time capsule, that's the time capsule. Inside that brick is a pot with a quilt in it . . . my quilt and my letter and other things from nineteen hundred. It was supposed to be opened in nineteen fifty. I remember it all."

Edna waited until the rain let up, then exited Hazel and walked over to the Queen and looked around. She hollered at Jeanette who was yet in the car, "We're not at the Queen. We're at that new place that's apparently a Queen, also. Al and Gertrude are going to be upset about this."

She returned to sit in the car. "My neck is

killing me from being wrenched around to drive. Are you ready to go?"

"What about the time capsule? We can't just leave it."

Edna, not believing the wild story, replied, "Aunt Jeanette, I think that thing out there has something to do with this second Daisy Queen. It must be new. I've never noticed it before."

"Well, go look at it, then," insisted Jeanette. You'll see a plaque on it telling something about when it was built and when it was to be opened."

Edna backed around the second Daisy Queen and stopped with the rear-mounted headlights shining directly on the structure. She got out and walked over to it, and there, under lichens and mosses, she could discern the outline of a plaque. She muttered, "This thing has been here a long time," then, she picked up a small piece of wood and wiped the plaque until she read aloud, "Hanghat 1900 TILL 1950." Then she said, "Must be a tomb. Wonder who's in it?" She looked up at the dog statue and thought that maybe it was a Spot's tomb—some famous Spot.

Edna returned to the car and regretfully informed Jeanette, "It's a tomb, I think a dog's tomb."

Jeanette, remembering the inscribed dates, said, "No, I'm sure it's a time capsule to be opened in nineteen fifty. I'm sure as I'm sitting here. . . . Am I sitting here? "

Edna replied, "Yes. You're here, Dear. That's the date on it alright. If that thing is real, we can open it tomorrow in time for the

Centennial Plus 10 celebration. This is just wonderful to happen right now. That thing must have been setting hidden in the underbrush all these years, and forgotten. It's providence to be rediscovered now. Hallelujah, wait till we tell everybody else."

Jeanette said, "My elbow hurts. I need a bottle of whatchamacallit."

Edna backed out of the parking lot and continued her errand.

At ten o'clock, exactly, the sign turned itself off, and the sky began to clear.

The next morning a crowd was sitting at the time capsule. Robert and his helpers broke through the bricks, and, sure enough, they found and extracted what looked like something that everybody agreed was either a coffin, a bomb, or a time capsule.

The cylinder was taken to the old, Wiggling Piglet grocery store, which had been unlocked and furnished with tables for the Centennial Plus 10 celebration.

Robert and Pauline used wrenches to loosen the bolts securing the lid, and, then, using a screwdriver, Pauline pried loose the lid. It opened with a hissing sound of air either entering or exiting.

Since Moody Marlin was out of town, Edna seemed to be in charge. All heads turned toward her, waiting for her to do something. She stepped forward, sniffed the opening, said it didn't smell moldy in the least, and then she removed the first item in the capsule—the 1000 year guarantee, which she read. Everybody sniffed the air and agreed that the thing had done its job.

Jeanette had declined coming to the opening of the capsule, saying she didn't exactly know why, but she had a feeling that something may upset her, and, anyway, she didn't feel well after being in all the damp weather last night.

The next item to be removed was the quilt. Edna and Erlene carefully spread it on a table. Everybody oohed and aahed at the beautiful autumn leaves on a tree which covered the quilt from edge to edge.

Edna, speaking in a singsong voice, addressed the assemblage, "I'm going to read the letter wrapped in the quilt."

The audience pulled their mazettes and other chairs closer.

She began speaking, "This quilt tells the story of the relationships of the original founders of Hanghat to each other, and it reveals that many of their children were sired by the same father, a man who lived in Louisiana and impregnated many of. . . ." Her voice trailed off, then she said, "Well, I declare. This is most unusual and unexpected."

Every soul there watched as she silently finished reading the two page letter, then the crowd waited expectantly for her to say something after she handed the letter to Erlene.

Edna continued speaking, "It's going to be hard to believe, but the leaves on the quilt tree tell who all has a common ancestor. He apparently talked himself into bed with many of the wives of the founders of our town. Just read the names written as leaves, if you want to. Maybe it's best we know. It certainly explains a lot of similar behavior on our parts. I always thought it was all the water, or something, or just our ways here on the uplift."

Jeanette's unsigned letter listed the traits that were passed on by whom the letter called, Sire, and among them she had listed, ". . . a powerful and compelling urge for women to conceive with different partners; a trait most common in all men."

The letter was passed around and read silently until each reader gasped while reading the part about the compelling urge and similar eccentricities. Many immediately stood up with a look on their face that said they never had really liked to sit all the time and only did it to fit in.

Pauline and Robert held each other close. They looked anxiously into each others eyes, then they went to stand around the quilt with a few others.

After a time Pauline stood back. Pale and faint she grabbed Robert and began to sob, "You and I have the same great great great grandfather. . . and worse, even probably closer relatives."

Robert, patting her on the back, asked, "What are we going to do about our June wedding?"

Pauline sobbed even louder and answered, barely getting the words out, "We shouldn't even k-k-kiss o-on the lips," then she began to bawl.

Robert tried to support her, but she pulled

away and found a chair to sit in. He watched his fiancee and realized that before she broke away to sit alone, he had felt like he was comforting a long lost cousin.

CHAPTER 30

The next morning all the phone lines on the uplift were still busy with conversations between newly discovered relatives, discussions about who looked like whom, and conjecture about other possible relationships. Some of the women who had become paranoid or guilt-ridden confessed to St. Thomas, who didn't seem to notice the heavier than usual volume.

It was May thirteenth and the centennial was the next day. Things had to be done, even with the town's familial emotions running wild. Many who had no relationship to Sire were suffering upset from suspicion and imagination. Others, who the quilt implied were related to Sire, were busy acting innocent or saying that one cannot help it if one is born that way.

At Fissile House Edna and Erlene were in a dither. When not taking phone calls from the despondent Pauline, or upset fornicators who were trying to determine if they were somehow implicated by the quilt, or calls about something to do with the festivities, they were jumping up and down in front of the range, trying to time perfect cake collapses.

Erlene was speaking on the phone, ". . . I'm trying to tell you, Maureen, that the quilt was put in that capsule in nineteen hundred, and there's no way your name could be on it. You're only thirty-five, or so. . . . Well, then, you're only twenty-nine, or so. Anyways, don't worry.

Gotta go. Bye."

Edna shouts from the kitchen, "This oven is set at four fifty. That's why the last two cakes are kinda weird."

Erlene high steps into the kitchen and asks, "What did you say? I just got off the phone with another woman wondering if their name was a leaf."

"I said you turned the oven up too high and I just turned it down."

Erlene took off her glasses and looked through them at arm's length, then said, "I'm seeing haloes ever since I cleaned them."

Edna replied with a disgusted voice, "Well, you probably smeared some cooking oil around on them. Use some dishwashing liquid and clean them before you burn the house down. . . . Wait, it smells like it's time to jump."

The two took their positions in front of the range and sniffed the air.

"It smells a little early to me," whispered Erlene.

"You don't have to whisper. The thing's not that sensitive. It takes both of us jumping to get one to fall. Tell me when you think it's ready."

Erlene began inhaling deeply every few seconds, but her raised arm, posed for signaling, didn't drop.

Edna, standing in a crouching position, ready to jump, asked, "Well, is it time?"

"I think I've hyperventilated," replied Erlene. "I need a paper bag before I faint."

Edna opened a drawer and handed a bag to her sister who began breathing into it. After a few breaths she removed the sack from her nose and sniffed the air, searching for the telltale aroma of jump time. She wobbled a bit, placed the bag over her mouth, inhaled and shouted, “It’s time,” and both women began jumping.

By noontime they had their routine perfected and were baking and jumping-down three puddin’ cakes at a time. Genevieve was helping place the cakes in cardboard boxes, and saying how much easier it was to walk across the living room since her rash went away.

Betty Joe had been phoning from the county hospital, but she had not been able to get through since every phone in Hanghat was busy most of the day. She finally got Jeanette on the line who told her something about everybody being upset and busy. Betty Joe considered that she was talking about preparations for the centennial. Before hanging up, she told Jeanette to call Edna, and tell her that she didn’t know whether she would be back that afternoon, or in the morning. Jeanette hung up, forgot about the call, and continued her search through the house for the bottle of medicine she had so needed during the heaviest and shortest rainstorm in years.

Robert, meanwhile, was staying occupied trying to keep his mind from dwelling upon the loss of true love, while hoping that such a distant relative would make no difference once he and Pauline had a chance to discuss what it all meant. Every hour he would drive past Pauline’s hoping to find her in the swing, beckoning him to stop, then telling him how silly it all had been, and that no old, long-dead grandfather was going to break them apart.

Sulking at home, he somehow remembered he had promised to help with the centennial preparations, and he forced himself to phone Fissile House, where Erlene said that they had a carload of Widow Ficher's Famous Puddin' Cakes to be delivered to the Wiggling Piglet.

Robert jumped into his pickup, drove over by Pauline's, then sadly drove to Fissile House, where he loaded the puddin' cakes and headed to the Wiggling Piglet. He unloaded the cakes and stayed to help with the preparations.

At six p.m. the Blue Carnival arrived in a column of vans and cars and trucks, all pulling house trailers. The lead vehicle driven by Mr. Blue, himself, who, following the directions he had been given in a letter from Betty Joe, turned left at the Daisy Queen and drove to the field at the end of the street and parked outside the walled compound.

The Ferris wheel was being assembled within fifteen minutes of their arrival, and tents began to spring up. Ponies let loose inside a rope corral were soon grazing calmly like they had been there for days.

At nine that evening, the Parableers had found the turnoff to Hanghat and were chugging up the steep section of the road above the bridge. In their station wagon were Mr. and Mrs. Johnson and their son, Gabriel, a fifteen year old smoker who played the role of supplicant to insure the allowance that maintained his addiction, and Mary Ann, their moody seventeen year old daughter who only continued as an actress in the service of the Lord as penitence for nightly stripping in front of her full length mirror to admire her nubile self while wishing some cute guy could see what she saw.

They pulled into town, and, following the directions he had been given, Mr. Johnson turned left at the Daisy Queen and drove till he came to a gate in a stone wall. He drove past the busy carnival scene and parked by other cars close to the gate. The family watched the activity in the field, and Mr. and Mrs. Johnson agreed that it meant they would possibly have the largest audience, ever. Then, loaded down with suitcases and props, the family walked to the gate and rang the bell.

Elgin Giddings opened the gate and asked, "You're not with that circus, are you?"

Mrs. Johnson, offended by the question, cooly replied that they had been invited by the SBA for the Return To The Garden show.

Elgin, who had just staggered in from the Tasting Room, failed to ask to see their Solar Bathers of America membership cards. He muttered, "Well la-de-da," then led them to an empty bungalow.

The Johnsons were asleep when Mr. Refren Coaxe and sixteen SBA members came through the gate with arm loads of garden tools. Refren was the national sales manager of the SBA. He was a short, persuasive man in his mid thirties, wiry with freckled skin, reddish blond hair, and bright green eyes that had talked many a person out of their clothes and into an SBA, three year membership at the Golden Tan level.

At eleven p.m. Betty Joe, with a pale Widow Ficher, arrived at Fissile House. Betty Joe went in, leaving the widow in the car until she returned with Edna and Erlene who helped the widow across the shagmire and into an empty bedroom where they tucked her in.

"Let me pour you some coffee," Erlene said to Betty Joe as they trudged through the living room.

The three sisters went into the kitchen where Edna said, "Betty Joe you won't believe what all has happened since you left. To begin with . . ."

Betty Joe interrupted, "I'd believe anything after that hospital. It was either get her out of there or go to her funeral. They damned near tested her to death. She was begging me to get her out, but by the time we could escape, she had been tested so much she was running low on blood and every other bodily fluid. She looked like a dried-up leaf when I got her to the Heespud City Queen, and got a milkshake and some food down her."

Erlene commented reassuringly, "Well, she looks good. Thank God you got her out of there. I think that bunch of nuts have tested more than one person to death."

The three, with their pinkies extended like

they should have little flags hanging from them, were sipping coffee.

Betty Joe asked, "What's it you were talking about that happened while I was gone?"

Edna and Erlene told the story, and while they spoke Betty Joe began to look worried.

"So," Erlene concluded, "your daughter is at home crying her eyes out, and Robert is beside himself with grief, and us, well, we've got the same great-great-grandfather on both sides of the family. Thank heavens Aunt Jeanette de-twitted us and broke us of that snicker."

Edna said, "I had always wondered why Aunt Jeanette was so strict about all that. Now, I understand."

Betty Joe stood up and paced the floor before speaking, "Well, that isn't the last surprise. I have another one. . . ."

Her revelation was delayed when a groaning, "Oh no!" came from the living room as their mother flopped onto the sofa. "I just can't step high enough at this late hour," said Genevieve, lying sprawled-out across the sofa.

Erlene and Betty Joe assisted her to a seat in the kitchen.

"I'm glad you're up, Mother," said Betty Joe, "I want you all to hear this. Bluntly, Pauline is not my daughter. I know she favors the family, but she is the child of a woman who was a knife thrower in the circus. Pauline comes from a long line of female, knife throwers dating back to the Renaissance in Alsace Lorraine. She was born to a woman who had an older daughter who was being abused by their Portuguese father, a circus acrobat and mean drunkard, who would drink, then force his wife and child to walk a tightrope strung between their trailer and his friend and fellow drunk, the circus strongman, Atlas Scruggs.

Pauline was born while the circus was wintering in Florida, just before beginning the spring tour. The father had spent the winter touring Brazil and didn't know Pauline was expected. When she was born, her mother pleaded with me to take the baby and raise her as my own, before her cruel father returned."

Genevieve commented, "Well, that explains why the child was so good at mumblety-peg. I never won a single time I played her."

"I tried to keep her away from knives," said Betty Joe, "I didn't know you had been teaching her mumblety-peg, Mother."

Genevieve answered, "You should have told us all this when you first returned."

"I didn't want her treated any different," said Betty Joe.

"Any different," Genevieve emphatically said, "all that would have amounted to is that I possibly would not have taught the child mumblety-peg."

Edna interjected, "What's important now is that we inform her gently, and if she truly loves Robert, then, this will be happy news, even if upsetting. Pauline is a strong girl, but I think we should all be with her for support when you tell her, Betty Joe."

"It's late," said Genevieve. "Betty Joe you

go on home, and if your daughter is awake, go ahead and tell her that she's not related to Robert, and you'll explain it all when we get there. Call us and we'll be early. The child is crying her eyes out."

At midnight a Phantom Lover installed a last part necessary for the success of the machination—a cigar box full of one dollar bills.

Robert was to be up all night in the Wiggling Piglet, fighting rats which were coming two and three at a time, trying to get at Widow Ficher's Famous Puddin' Cakes. The sheriff dropped by the Piglet to see if everything was going smoothly and to check the premises for any hint of Phantom Lover activity. The sheriff then remained long enough to kill a dozen of the rapacious vermin with a 22 revolver loaded with rat shot.

Robert threw the carcasses out the back doors, then lay down on the table next to the puddin' cakes. He spent the night dozing and waking, sleeping little, watching for rats, and pining for his lost love.

By two a.m. the campfire at the Blue Carnival was glowing embers beside a Ferris wheel spinning slowly back and forth in the breeze.

Refren Coaxe had become the big loser in a game of dress poker, and, fully clothed in a suit and tie, headed to bed in a bad mood.

CHAPTER 31

Dawn came to the big day. The parade was to begin at ten a.m. at the intersection of Main and 2nd, then go up Main to 11th, turn left at the Queen, and end at the carnival in the fair grounds—a distance of about a mile.

The Main Street business area was decorated with banners, and red, white, and blue crepe wrapped street lamps, each with a colorful flag flying from the top. A sign in front of the Wiggling Piglet building read, "Chairs, Arts & Crafts, & Hanghat's Famous Pudding Cakes."

Al and Gertrude had decorated the Queen, and had opened at eight a.m. to serve the crowd lining the parade route. Their hamburger patties were tight and stacked high in the fridge, and the soft-serve machine was ready and waiting to fill cones and plastic cups with the Queen-style, ice cream-like, custard-like, Daisy treat.

Motor driven and horse drawn floats formed a line along 2nd Street from West Side to Main, and waited for the start signal from Moody Marlin who had overslept after a late return from vacation.

It had been four in the morning when the Marlin family drove into town and past the new, unlit Queen without noticing it, but, then, in daylight the new Queen was an attraction and a wonder. A crowd of Uplifters, including Moody, gathered around it, taking turns peeking in the windows.

Moody was peering into the building with his hands held to the sides of his face to shield reflections, when he felt a tug on his arm. He looked around to see Llano Bandera.

Llano excitedly said, “Mr. Moody, there is no carnival at the fair grounds. It’s over at the end of Third Street, and there is nobody there but blue people, and I don’t think they are painted.”

Moody drove over to the carnival where he soon found out what had happened to cause the mistake. He knew he had to improvise, and he knew the businessmen expected the parade to take the route past Hanghat’s pride—the cleaned and decorated Main Street.

He returned to the head of the parade and got behind the wheel of the lead vehicle, a white, 1965 Cadillac convertible with the parade prince and princess sitting on the top of the back of the rear seat. Then, at ten-thirty, he began driving up Main Street, followed by the nine member Hanghat High Hedgehog Band marching ahead of a block-long line of floats ranging from a horse-drawn wagon full of people sitting in hay and wearing western clothes, to a hitherto unseen flying saucer-like contraption which was about ten feet in diameter, with a flat area on top about the size of a bed.

Earlier that morning Dr. Bertram had waved a signal flag to start the catfish catching contest at Train Lake. The Centennial Plus Ten committee had reluctantly included the catfish contest at the bottom of the ad in the Heespud City, the Haygap, and the Phleville newspapers, and fifty fishermen had shown up to try for the hundred dollar prize the doctor was offering in an effort to assure that the pet-eating menace was surely caught.

Train Lake was muddy from the recent rains, and two feet of water was pouring over the locomotive dam between the cab and the tender. Fifty hooks were in the lake, but there was no action until the great fish surfaced in the middle of the lake. It swam around the floats supporting the baited hooks, but the fish, which had eaten a duck the afternoon before, was not interested in the assortment of livers and stink baits the catfish fishermen swore by.

Dr. Bertram paced the bank, becoming more frustrated with time, then the fish swam close to where the doctor stood. He saw the fish as taunting him, then in a move that startled the fifty fishermen and the casual fish, the old doctor jumped onto the back of the fish and grabbed his arms around it.

Crazed, he shouted, “I’ll teach you to eat my dog, you son-of-a-bitch,” and held on as the fish began swimming toward its lair.

The man on the fish sped through the water like a fast moving rowboat, but before the frantic fish could dive, the two spun over and the doctor was now beneath the fish. The fish couldn’t steer or dive. Dr. Bertram held on, and the fish splashed and writhed until it was in the current pouring out of the lake, and gone over the dam with Dr. Leander Bertram still attached.

The doctor was pulled from the creek, but

the fish escaped in the creek, to finally belly-flop down the cataracts leading down the side of the uplift, and ending up in the Bratity, where he could still be spotted, once in a while, until the café down by the bridge offered an all-you-can-eat catfish dinner special that ran a full month.

At eight that morning, the Parableers came out of their bungalow, saw naked people walking about, smiling and waving and shouting welcomes and good mornings. Mrs. Johnson grabbed her son and daughter by their arms and ushered them back into the bungalow.

She gasped and asked, "What in the world of God is going on here? Did you see that, Honey?" she asked Mr. Johnson, who was peering out a window.

"They're all naked; not a stitch on, not a stitch," he declared.

The son, Gabriel, said, "Well this is supposed to be the Garden of Eden, and this is supposed to be the return to it; that's why they're naked, that's the way God had it."

Mary Ann moved to a window and saw a young man and woman pass just outside the bungalow. She suddenly wanted to throw off her clothes and join them.

Her mother grabbed her away and looked for a curtain to close, but there wasn't one.

She then went to the door and cracked it enough to shout at a passerby carrying a rake, "Excuse me, ma'am, is there something unusual going on?"

The woman answered, "It sure is, Honey,"

and continued walking while saying, "Gotta get back to the garden. Are you coming out soon? The show must go on," the naked woman added with a laugh, but Mrs. Johnson took the expression literally and assumed the woman was talking about the Parableer's performance.

Mr. and Mrs. Johnson were Baptist thespians. Baptist, because a Baptist, family friend had talked them into Baptistry, and thespians, because both had descended from limelighters and vaudevillians. They had inherited the urge to perform, but both were short on talent and had to settle for corny, religious skits—the only outlet they could find for their thespian urges.

The two huddled and mulled over the dilemma. Should they strip and go out that door and put on a show? What would the children think?

Gabriel and Mary Ann had snuck back to the window. Gabriel saw a smoker on the patio of the next bungalow. The smoker lit a cigarette, exhaled, and walked away leaving his pack of cigarettes on a patio table. The smoke drifted in and past Gabriel, and he inhaled as much as he could, then sensed that he was on the verge of having a nicotine fit.

Mary Ann kept hoping to see some more naked young men, and she furtively moved her head around the opening trying to catch a glimpse of a particular couple who had passed by. She began to think that she should seize the opportunity to be seen in the altogether, at last, then pray like a nun at the Vatican until she felt forgiven.

Frustrated, they both slipped out a back door while their parents were discussing the situation, and the two walked right into Refren Coaxe.

Refren commanded, “Oh no you don’t,” and held out his arms to bar their way. “You must be the children of the new members the caretaker told me about. You must have read the rules by now. Clothing is not optional in the resort, so get back inside and get undressed, and tell your parents that Refren Coaxe wants to see them. I’ll be in the garden.”

Mary Ann delivered the message as, “We just ran into our first naked reverend. He said he was Reverend Cox, and he’s wondering where you are.”

Mrs. Johnson slinked to the window and looked out again, then shouted, “My God, Gabriel is naked as the day he was born, and is walking into the bushes behind the cabin next door.”

Gabriel had stripped, gone to the next bungalow, snatched a cigarette and matches, and was going off to grab a long-needed smoke.

Refren Coaxe barged in while the three remaining Johnsons were huddled, staring out the window.

“Are you people coming out and join in, or what. We need all the help we can get to have the garden ready by this afternoon. The reason we’re here is the garden.”

Mrs. Johnson looked helpless as she eyed

her first naked reverend, then she stuttered a second, raised her eyes and meekly asked, "Is it okay if we put on a performance after it's dark tonight. We've got an inflatable apple tree with a real apple and an inflatable snake and everything, but I don't think we're up to an afternoon performance. We'll need time to adjust to being in the Garden of Eden like God made it."

Mr. Johnson asked, "Will we be putting on fig leaves after I take a bite of the apple, Reverend?"

"I don't think you can find a fig tree. Anyways, provocative attire is outside the rules of the SBA," retorted Refren, "unless it's theatrical, of course." He stepped toward them and into a shaft of morning light which blazed his green eyes as he said "Right now, get out of your clothes and come and help."

Mr. and Mrs. Johnson, intimidated, nervously turned to see how Mary Ann was doing; expecting her to be appalled, but, instead seeing her clothes on her bed, and her gone.

They heard her happy voice through the window, "I'm outside just the way God made me."

The two gulped and hesitatingly undressed, then they skulked out the door and tiptoed bush to bush until they were discovered by Refren, who, looking them straight in the eye, and never dropping his eyes, handed the pair a hoe each and turned, saying to follow him.

At the garden, nobody seemed to show any sign of lust for, or interest in, the two embarrassed novices, except that the others said, hello, or, good morning, and continued to react like the Johnsons were the fully-clothed couple in the painting, American Gothic, and not as who the Johnsons saw themselves—two pasty, freshly denuded relatives of Snow White.

After working in the naked group for awhile, someone yelled, “Pool cool down,” and everybody dropped their gardening tools and ran off into the bushes.

The Johnsons stood in place until one of the men reappeared and said, “Come on, it’s time for a swim.”

The couple found their two children in the swimming pool. Neither Mary Ann nor Gabriel could be talked out of the pool when the work party returned to the garden, and by lunch time, a relaxed Mr. and Mrs. Johnson felt like they should have been nudists before this.

That same morning that the Parableers were adjusting to nudity, Betty Joe awakened Pauline, and tenderly admitted to her that she was adopted, and she was not in any way related to Robert.

Pauline alternated between crying from shock and crying from happiness, then she and her mother drove off to find Robert and tell him the strange good news. They found his pickup and were told that he had spent the night in the Piglet. They phoned his house and his mother said he hadn’t been in since the day before.

Robert had left the Piglet at sunrise, and he had sleepily walked to the new location of the city hall trailer just a block away, where he was asleep on a sofa.

Betty Joe said that she had some things to do, said for Pauline to keep searching for Robert, and she walked off toward the gathering parade.

Now back to eleven a.m., the time that the parade had turned the corner at the original Queen. Upon turning onto 11th Street, the wagon tongue had come loose from the axle of the hay ride. The team of two horses stood silently while the wagon rolled to a stop in the parking lot of the Queen.

It took twenty-five minutes to reattach the tongue, a time during which the school band and members of the crowd rushed the Queen for burgers and custard.

The parade then continued down 11th, turned left on Front Street, and continued back north to 3rd where a crowd was waiting for its arrival.

Once in the thick of the crowd, the naked Phantom Lovers inside the flying saucer float had planned on exiting a hatch in the platform, wearing only Lone Ranger masks. There they would copulate quickly in full view, then throw out a flurry of dollar bills, and, while the crowd pushed forward fighting for the money, re-enter the saucer, rapidly don their clothes just like they had rehearsed, then exit by a trap door underneath the saucer, and melt into the crowd.

But, while the wagon tongue was being reattached, a young naked smoker was at the rear of the SBA compound, smoking another pilfered cigarette, when he heard his father calling and looking for him. Gabriel quickly flicked the still lit butt over a bush, where it landed in a large mound of dry leaves just raked up from inside a pavilion and dumped.

When the parade was three blocks away from the SBA and the carnival, a thick cloud of white smoke began to fill the area inside the walls of the SBA.

Coughing, choking nudists were forced out the front gate just as the saucer stopped. Inside the saucer the Phantom Lovers heard the crowd outside cheer and shout. They threw open the hatch and climbed onto the platform, and stood there naked and masked and erect and horny as rabbits. They saw nothing but the backs of the crowd, as curiosity lured their would-be audience toward a scene of naked people and smoke pouring out the gate of the SBA.

Sheriff Marshal was running toward the mass of nudity, and he was thinking how come it was that he never suspected all the Baptists, but only the caretaker, who he now suspected was the mastermind of a nest of exhibitionists who probably had a horse and Lady Godiva wig somewhere inside their compound, and ready to ride out. Yes, the sheriff was about a dozen detective novels over the sanity line.

Mr. Blue and Facile, in full feathered costume as, Azule the Blue Ostrich, had yelled, "Hey, Rube," the trade's call for help, and every carny joined in to form a line between the nudists and the crowd.

From the top seats of the paused, Ferris wheel, riders saw a bunch of tanned, naked people milling about between a wall and a semicircle of blue people in blue uniforms and costumes. Huddled against the wall were four, pasty white figures, looking bewildered. An intrigued and titillated, but cautious crowd, stayed back from the blue people like they were afraid they would be grabbed, stripped, and thrown into the herd of corralled nudity.

The disappointed Phantom Lovers got back into the saucer and drove it away; jabbering to each other and wondering what in the hell had just happened. As they drove up 2nd toward Main, the last horse blanket was tossed out onto the side of the road, along with two Lone Ranger masks.

They had both come to the same conclusion as one of them said, “What’s the use, hell there’s naked people everywhere. The thrill is gone. Tell me where you want out. I’m driving back to where I’m safe from all this.”

“Let me out behind the Piglet.”

CHAPTER 32

The smoldering pile of leaves was extinguished, and the Solar Bathers of America regained their refuge, shutting the gate behind them. It was two o'clock and the carnival was at last back to business as normal, except for a long line of customers waiting to ride the Ferris wheel because it afforded a view of the other side of the wall. The view was only of flora, however, because the fauna had quit the garden and were at the swimming pool, which was hidden from the wheel's view. The Johnson family was behind their bungalow, practicing for their performance and wondering what could serve as a substitute fig leaf to wear after Adam bites into sin.

Robert had awakened at one o'clock, hungry enough to consume two of Gertrude's burgers, with a large fries and coke, so he walked to the Queen; leaving his pickup back in the Piglet parking lot.

Main was crowded, and so was the Queen. Only ten of the Widow Ficher's Famous Puddin' Cakes remained unsold. Erlene had been selling the cakes while Edna, Betty Joe, and Genevieve with Pauline, had sought Robert.

Edna was at the table speaking with Erlene when Pauline came in and exclaimed, "I haven't seen him anywhere. His pickup is out in the parking lot, but he's gone."

Edna asked, "Where's your grandmother?"

Oh, she's sitting on the bench outside."

"And your mother?" asked Edna.

Pauline replied, "I haven't seen her since this morning."

Erlene quipped, "This is the first I've seen hide nor hair of any of you in the last few hours. Watch the cakes and chairs while I go pee. I need a break. And," she whispered aside, "keep an eye on that man. I think he might be a little tetched."

She was referring to a short, round man sweating in a suit and tie, and who had been inspecting a mazette, placing and removing the rockers, and alternately rocking and sitting.

The man got up, leaving the mazette in the rocker mode, and approached Pauline and asked her, gesturing toward the chair, "Are these made locally?"

Pauline replied, "Yes," and gestured toward Edna. "My aunt can tell you about them."

Edna and the man walked over to the chair sales area and continued to converse.

Erlene returned, just as Betty Joe entered the building.

Pauline asked, "Did you see him anywhere. His pickup is in the lot outside, but he's not anywhere."

Betty Joe said, "I just came from the Queen. The Samsons said he had eaten there and said he was going to the carnival. He's probably there now."

The group sat and waited for Edna to finish talking with the suited man. Eventually she came over, folding a sheet of paper and placing it in her purse.

Betty Joe spoke, “Robert is over at the carnival, and I would like us all to be there when he’s told about Pauline’s not being related.”

Edna said, “We’ll have to walk the four blocks. There’s no place to park over there that’s much closer than here, and I don’t want to back through all that traffic.”

Genevieve said that she would mind the cakes and the chairs, and told them to go.

They found Robert in line for the Ferris wheel. He came over to them and stood next to Erlene, who was furthest from Pauline. He didn’t know how to greet his ex-fiancee, and he didn’t think it was proper, anymore, to just walk up and stand close to her, so he just nodded hello from a distance.

Betty Joe repeated the story of how Pauline happened to be adopted, and when she had finished the tale, Robert asked if it was really true, and how it was that Pauline looked so much like Betty Joe.

“I won’t feel like I can love Pauline in the way I did unless I know for sure that we’re not related.”

Pauline added, “I feel the same. I mean I still love you, Robert, but I must put to rest this feeling of being your sister, or cousin.”

“I can prove it,” said Betty Joe. “I mean, Pauline can prove it. I hear there’s a knife thrower at the carnival. To help you both understand, Pauline, you’ll throw knives.”

Pauline protested, “But, I’ve never thrown knives except playing mumblety-peg with

Grandma."

Betty Joe replied, "Don't worry, I know the ability comes naturally to the women in your family."

Betty Joe asked a blue clown for the whereabouts of Mr. Blue, and the clown pointed to a blue man wearing a blue top hat and blue, Arabic style robes and slippers. Betty Joe went to him and introduced herself as the Betty Joe Dumas who had corresponded with him. Then, she told him what she wanted to do.

Mr. Blue looked at Pauline, then called Facile over. "Look at this girl, my Dear, and tell me who she resembles."

Mrs. Blue stared at Pauline then said, "I don't know, but she does look familiar."

"Think of a knife thrower," said Mr. Blue.

"Oh, yes," replied Mrs. Blue, removing an ostrich feather from the corner of her mouth, ". . . she favors Madam Lilva from Circus Minimus." She looks at Pauline and asks, "Are you related to her, my dear?"

Pauline replies, "I've just been told that she is my mother. Have you seen her recently?"

"I heard, but I'm not sure, that she was teaching throwers in St. Augustine, Florida at the Dangerous And Deadly Acts School. It's in the phone book there. My older brother, Dificil, God rest his soul, almost learned the art of snake charming at that school."

Betty Joe said, "Mr. Blue, I need to prove that Madam Lilva is this girl's mother. Would you allow her to throw knives at the Wheel of

Possible Tragedy if we use balloons instead of a person?"

"But of course, Betty Joe. It would be no inconvenience at all. Especially since everybody is in line for the Ferris wheel."

The group walked toward a tent while Mr. Blue told Betty Joe how interested he was in returning to Hanghat every year and setting up his Ferris wheel in the same spot. He told her that it was making the carnival a profit beyond anything he had expected.

Inside the tent, Betty Joe and the carnival's knife throwing team, The Incredible Coupers, fixed air-filled balloons inside the outline of a body on the Wheel of Possible Tragedy.

The Coupers then told Pauline where to stand, and the male, knife thrower threw a switch which started the wheel spinning.

Pauline asked, "Shouldn't somebody at least show me how to hold the knives?"

Betty Joe replied, "Just do what feels natural. Just watch the wheel and concentrate, and wait for instinct to tell you what to do. The moment will come, relax, you'll know what to do."

Pauline, motionless and breathing slow, deep breaths, stared at the wheel turning at a steady rate. Betty Joe and the others looked on as the anticipation grew.

Three minutes had passed when Pauline imagined that the wheel had suddenly stopped spinning, then the tent and everything and everyone in it began spinning—all whirled round and round, except her, the table of knives before her, and the wheel, frozen, twenty feet away. Unthinking, she grabbed and hurled knife after knife until sixteen blades outlined the balloons, without popping even one.

Upon throwing the last knife, she again saw the wheel as the only thing spinning. Then, her mind began to carousel with flashes of thoughts about her birth mother, and her mother, and Robert, and faces she knew but had never seen.

Robert was there to catch her as she fainted, and she felt safe and content in his arms when she came back to consciousness.

She asked, "What happened? How did I do?"

He helped her stand. He pointed to the wheel and said, "Look. It's obvious that you and I are from different families."

Their original lover's love returned and they embraced.

POSTLUDE

By May 17, 1971, the second Daisy Queen was gone from Hanghat, and by the end of May, a second Queen had been built on the southwest corner of Main and 3rd Street in Haygap, Texas, where it was supposed to have been built.

Al and Gertrude were very glad to see it being trucked down Main and out of town, and were to enjoy the rewards of being the only Queen in town for the rest of their working years, at which time they retired to Florida. There they lived as close to a Queen as possible, so they could walk to it, and enjoy the fare without having to prepare it.

Volunteer fire chief, Terry LeConte, had discovered honeyberry bushes while inside the Solar Bathers of America during the smoldering leaf incident. Refren Coaxe allowed a group of older Hanghatters inside to dig up some of the bushes for transplanting, and he agreed to give that year's honeyberries to the town, to be used for seeds to replant the uplift with the area's official fruit. Refren demanded that anybody who came into the compound had to remove their clothing, and after much debate, the diggers of the honeyberry bushes were selected by a hot and heavy ten minutes of rock, paper, scissors.

Miss Pauline Dumas became Mrs. Robert Olin Beer that June in a Catheran ceremony, sitting in mazettes, and wearing garlands of honeyberry branches. The couple said their, I

Do's, and the litany of, I Won't's, which Reverend Beer had included in the Catheran, marriage ceremony after the disclosures of the quilt and letter. Then the couple left for a Mexican honeymoon.

With the passage of the years, Hanghat set frozen, slowly sublimating away, like many other small, Texas towns too distant from a metropolis to be an exurb. For a few years the secret building was used to manufacture mazettes for the sweating man in the suit and tie who, it turned out, was a buyer for a furniture distributor. Honeyberry preserves made a comeback, and the uplift became known in the tri-county area as the Honeyberry Capital of the World, according to the last repaint of the sign at the cutoff.

Hanghat at of the end of the twentieth century was the home of three hundred people living on retirement and social security. The Queen held a regular, Wednesday morning coffee club that was well attended.

The once, spanking-new brick business area existed in its glory days only on a painting hanging in Tall Texas Antiques—the former Collage Department Store. Prints of the painting were for sale, along with prints of two more—"Wandering Albatross Sitting Atop Honeyberry Bush" and "Wandering Albatross Sitting On Top Mr. Mouvoir's Head."

"Wandering Albatross Sitting On Fissile House" was still above the mantle in the living room of Fissile House, now occupied by Robert and Pauline and visited by their children and grandchildren. Robert and Pauline owned both antique stores in Hanghat, and were making a decent income. They had no idea that the collection of nondescript paintings in the Fissile House attic were all the work of a genius, and that the works, when eventually exhibited, would astound the art world with an entirely new school of metaphor-less art to be named, Noumenonism.

Today, the uplift sets miles from the closest interstate. But, if you're ever driving parallel to I-35 somewhere between Austin and Dallas, and you see a distant lightning storm raging so far away that you cannot hear the thunder, it is probably over on the uplift. But, don't go looking for Hanghat unless you have the time to search for, and the good luck to find, the cutoff from that sneaky, decreasing radius, reverse cambered curve.

THE END